Caught

Gold Hockey #15

Elise Faber

CAUGHT
BY ELISE FABER
Newsletter sign-up

This is a work of fiction. Names, places, characters, and events are fictitious in every regard. Any similarities to actual events and persons, living or dead, are purely coincidental. Any trademarks, service marks, product names, or named features are assumed to be the property of their respective owners, and are used only for reference. There is no implied endorsement if any of these terms are used. Except for review purposes, the reproduction of this book in whole or part, electronically or mechanically, constitutes a copyright violation.

Gold Hockey Series

***Gold Hockey* (all stand alone)**
Blocked
Backhand
Boarding
Benched
Breakaway
Breakout
Checked
Coasting
Centered
Charging
Caged
Crashed
A Gold Christmas
Cycled
Caught
Cap

ONE

CHARLIE

He wove his way through the bowels of the arena.

An unfortunate description.

But he was waiting for his sister, Scarlett, or for one of his friends, Fanny, Kaydon, or Mandy.

They all worked for the Gold—his sister in the publicity department, Fanny as a skating coach, Mandy as a trainer, and Kaydon...well, that big ball of deliciousness was a player who was currently killing it on the ice—or had been, anyway, until the buzzer had rung fifteen minutes before.

Now the game was over, and Charlie was still hiding.

Hiding like he'd been doing from the moment he'd seen—

A bolt of pain through his middle.

Why couldn't he spot any of the people he wanted to see?

As opposed to the one person he was hiding from in the aforementioned bowels, trying to *avoid* seeing.

Ji-Ho.

His ex had taken a transfer and was now working in the San Francisco office of the tech company they'd both been with when they'd first met in South Korea. Met being the weakest word possible for it. Rather they'd had an instant connection. Chemistry. Banter. And...Charlie had fallen deeply.

But...it hadn't ended well.

He'd tried to quit, his boss hadn't been happy to let him go, and eventually Charlie had gotten a transfer here to San Francisco (mostly because Scar was here and he loved his sister, but also because he had gotten close to her friend Fanny when he visited, so it had made sense to move and be close to them both).

A fresh start.

Putting the messy situation with Ji-Ho behind him, leaving the nightmare HR scenario in the past, and just...beginning again.

And now he'd been living his life, finally settling in and feeling like himself again, when he'd turned his head and saw his ex at the Gold game that evening.

Next door to where he was sitting.

Charlie hadn't been in that *same* concrete box, perched high above the ice—thankfully. Even though he worked for the same company, the same branch of the organization as Ji-Ho, Charlie had been in the Gold's box, Ji-Ho in RoboTech's. But it had been near enough. *Too* near. He'd worked closely with Ji-Ho in Korea—

Love. A broken heart. Despair. Now...alone. So *fucking* alone.

Needless to say, he'd been avoiding Ji-Ho since he'd heard of his ex's transfer to the .

But that wasn't why he hadn't been in the RoboTech's box (hell, he wouldn't have thought his ex would *ever* go to a hockey game...though now that he knew, he'd be avoiding the RoboTech box like the plague). Fanny had invited him to hang out with her while she worked, and since his sister worked for the Gold, he usually sat in the team box when he came to catch a game, teasing Fanny, watching Scar do her publicist thing, smiling as she mooned over her gorgeous hockey player man...*fiancé?*

He wasn't quite sure where she and Kaydon stood. Kay never took off a plastic Hello Kitty ring his sister had proposed with, but Scar wasn't sporting a diamond, and though they'd moved in together, neither of them appeared to be moving toward setting any wedding dates.

It was just...a love fest.

All the time.

Add in Fanny—another ex (if having one date together and becoming friends could be an ex, which was a story for a different night, but *still*)—and her husband Brandon. Scar and Kaydon. Mandy and Blane. Brit and Stefan. Coop and Calle. Char and Logan. Dani and Ethan. Mia and—

Well, the point was that there weren't a lot of prospects for a single man on this team.

Even less so when he considered that none of the single men on the team were bi or gay or interested in a semi-scrawny (at least compared to them) redhead bisexual man who'd had his heart broken and had run away like a baby because of it. *And* all the women he knew were paired up.

Because if they were single and interested, he would be *such* a catch, right?

Right.

And yes, that was sarcasm.

So anyway, he'd been sitting on the chair next to Scar, amazed at all the things she did at once and handled with aplomb, and he'd turned, and...

Ji-Ho.

In the next box over.

Charlie had wanted to run, to hide, to pretend he hadn't seen his ex.

But...pride.

So, he had lifted his chin, held his stare steady when their eyes had locked, and...he'd pretended that his heart wasn't still cracked.

Still shattered.

It wouldn't have worked out. He knew that now. But, fuck, he'd moved halfway around the world to be closer to the man he'd met at a conference, a man he'd thought might be something permanent, and they'd ended up...

As a disaster.

Now Ji-Ho was here. *Why* was he here?

Charlie wasn't about to find out. Not when the man had cheated on him. Not when he'd sabotaged Charlie's work. Not when...he'd done so much more than that, had *been* so much worse. And that wasn't even counting that he hadn't treated Charlie's heart with the same care every couple in this strange cornucopia of happy endings treated their partners' hearts.

Charlie wanted *that*.

Care.

To receive it. To give it.

And now he knew he deserved it.

"*I* deserve it," he whispered, hoping that if he said it out loud that he would finally believe it. Sighing, he pushed through the door to a room that was usually empty, intending to take a moment to get that sentiment through his thick, still-sort-of-pining-for-Ji-Ho-even-though-that-was-fucking-stupid-because-Ji-Ho-was-a-total-jerk skull.

However, instead of making his way through the door, he collided with something firm and huge...

And gold.

No *Gold*. As in, Goldie.

The #GlitteryGoldieGuano in the flesh. *Er*. In the *costume*.

The giant poop-shaped mascot that had somehow become—much to Scar's chagrin—a fan-favorite. With their collision, the poop—well, the costume performer inside all that gold material—tipped over backward, landing with an *oof* that made Charlie cringe and rush forward, kneeling at the glittering dump's side.

The triangular piece at the top had popped off, rolled across the room.

"Are you oka—"

His question froze in his throat. His heart seized.

Because when the top of that giant golden poop had fallen off, it revealed...

The most beautiful woman he'd ever seen.

Two

KACEE

She'd somehow gotten outside.

The suit definitely was hot and disorienting and it was challenging to see where she was going—hence the whole crashing into things...*thing*—but she thought she knew her way around by now.

There shouldn't have been a wall there.

And she shouldn't be on her back staring up at the bright blue sky.

For one, wasn't the game at night?

For another—

"Are you okay?"

She blinked, the bright blue sky faded—or maybe it coalesced, came together into the gorgeous blue irises of the gorgeous man leaning over her.

Red hair, but not a coppery red. A deep red that was almost mahogany.

In fact, it *was* mahogany, so much so that she would bet that if she put his head right up next to one of the cabinets she'd recently made, the stain on that wood would match his hair.

"Hello?" he asked gently.

Another blink and she focused.

Or at least, she focused enough to try and sit up.

Which...

Didn't go well.

Because her trying to sit up was less sitting and more lurching and—

Crack.

Her skull collided with the man's and then instead of it being daytime and her staring up at a beautiful blue sky, she was seeing stars.

Swimming around the edges of her vision.

Sparking.

Fingers on her forehead, smoothing over the throbbing spot there. "Easy, sweetheart." Then an arm was around her shoulders, sitting her back up—minus the head cracking this time. He hauled her to her feet. "Where's the zipper on this thing?" he murmured.

And what she normally wouldn't give to hear that question from a man.

She was single.

So. Single.

So single she was half convinced that she'd find herself in a situation where a man actually wanted to take off her panties and instead of her displaying her feminine wares—porn-star style, when she spread her legs—a cloud dust would poof out instead.

Also, it probably wouldn't surprise anyone that she was nowhere near a porn star in bed.

(Which may be contributing to her whole single status...but *cêst la vie*).

"Did I concuss you?"

Kacee shook her head. "I...um...no..." She rewound, remembered what he asked, and lifted her arm, yanking back the flap of fabric that was velcroed in place and hid the zipper. Then she grabbed the tab, yanked *that*, and pretty soon the side of Goldie was gaping open in a way that would terrify any child who saw her.

And...it terrified *her.*

Because...she'd forgotten.

About The Funk.

He stepped close.

She'd started to slip her head out the top when that funky smell began to hit the edges of her nose. "Oh, fuck," she breathed, trying to shove her head back in, tugging at the top of the costume.

Zip it.

Zip it *now.*

Zip it before The Funk—*her* funk born of hours in the Goldie costume that was made of all variety of synthetic fabrics, none of which breathed, and all of which clung to the material. In the worst way possible. Because being a mascot was hard work. It involved dancing, running, skipping, shuffling across the ice and trying not to eat it. It involved *stairs.* Loads of stairs. Running up them to boogie with a cute little kid. Shimmying down them to give away a T-shirt or twenty. Prowling through the concourse taking pictures with college kids, with littler ones, with...parents.

Because everyone loved Goldie.

But if the fabric that made up Goldie actually breathed, actually allowed the stink that she'd gotten used to, to escape...then there would be no Goldie love.

It would be a Goldie quarantine.

Which was what she needed to do right at that moment.

Her fingers scrabbled for the tag of the zipper, but she was doing that at the same time she was trying to shove her head back inside.

"Ow!" she hissed, her head-shoving stalled when her hair got caught on...something—

The teeth of the zipper? The snap to keep the top of Goldie together? The Velcro that hid the opening? Satan's pitchfork because he was a big ole asshole and wanted to torment her?

"Um...you okay?"

She was not okay.

Very *not* okay.

So *not* okay that she tried to shuffle away from the man, but she did it letting go of the zipper, which meant that any progress made in containing The Funk was abated as she battled with her hair.

Her gaze skated over the room, over to her desk.

Scissors!

Except the desk was empty.

Except...she had a sewing kit there.

And, yeah, she liked her hair, but if there was ever a moment to lop the fuck out of her hair, this was it. Kacee would extract those tiny scissors from the little pink kit, and she'd saw away at her hair.

Anything to save her from *this*.

From this beautiful man smelling her funk.

She waddled toward her desk, knocking into her chair, tumbling a small table, listening to it crash to the floor, and not caring.

It was getting that sewing kit or die.

Her base layer—black leggings, a tight black tank top—were soaked through, clinging to her skin and contributing to her current odiferous situation. Her hair was stuck on whatever she was stuck on. Goldie was gaping open.

And the smell...it was all around.

And suddenly...that man was there.

"Let me help you."

She lurched away, her desk rattling. "No."

He stopped and her eyes hit his, but just for a moment before drifting over his face, lest she get lost in his pretty blue-sky gaze again. A straight nose, a defined jaw dusted with reddish-brown stubble, lighter than his hair and giving her serious sexy lumberjack feels. Laugh lines around his eyes, a hint of pink on his cheeks, and...a faint shadow on his forehead.

Probably from *her* forehead crashing into his.

Shit.

"Do you want me to get someone else to help?" He shifted closer still, definitely in The Funk range now.

"No," she said again, abandoning her hair, abandoning her scrabbling for the sewing kit, and returning to zipper yanking.

Silence.

The man stopped, hands up. "Am I making you uncomfortable?" he asked gently.

"I—"

She *was* uncomfortable, and it was because of him...but it also wasn't him. It was her and her smell, her sweaty clothes, her knack for being a complete and utter wreck. "No," she finished quietly. "I'm fine."

Blue eyes on hers, as though he were studying her answer, deciphering whether it was a lie or truth. In the end, he must have gone for the latter.

But then he bent and reached for her hair.

Nose *all* up in The Funk Zone.

"*No!*"

He froze, lifted a brow. "You want to remain in this position?"

Well, no. She'd rather saw her hair off than be in this position, hence the whole searching for her sewing kit and the tiny scissors within thing. But she'd rather remain in that position if it meant that she could stop this man from experiencing The Funk.

Which was why she said, "I'm fine." And then paired that with clutching at the opening, trying futilely to contain the smell.

That other brow joined the first, but he didn't comment, just slid back a step. "I'll leave you to it then," he said softly.

She nodded, teeth nibbling into her bottom lip, not missing his gaze going there.

Maybe he couldn't smell her? Maybe even though her nose was burning from her own odor, she'd done a good job of containing the scent—

The door crashed open.

Scarlett popped her head in, and within one second, her expression said clearly that Kacee hadn't done a good job containing the odor. Nope, not in the least. Scar coughed and retreated a step into the hallway. "I'll just get the spray." Her gaze drifted from Kacee and the costume to the man. "Char? What are you doing here?"

He grinned. "Trying to take down your mascot apparently." He moved to where the top of Goldie's head had rolled as a result of their collision. He scooped it up, set it on the desk. "I'll head out."

Finally.

Relief slid through her.

Short-lived, it turned out.

"Oh no," Scar said. "I'm getting the spray, but Charlie, you are going to take care of it."

Kacee's eyes went wide. "I—no—"

"Scar," Charlie warned, his gentle gaze drifting from hers to Scarlett's. "I don't think that—"

"It's perfect," Scarlett says. "You have no sense of smell, so you can help her with…" This was the point she trailed off, thankfully, though Kacee wasn't too thankful because mentally she supplied something like, "*you can help her without gagging.*"

So thankful wasn't huge on her list of things, not at that moment.

It was, however, *there.*

Namely, because of the *no sense of smell* thing.

"Right," Scar recovered, not finishing that sentence because she wasn't an asshole. "I'll get the spray, Kace. Charlie, you're on Goldie duty."

Kacee opened her mouth, to say something, to say *anything*, but the door clicked closed and Scar was gone.

Leaving her with Charlie and his handsome face, piercing blue eyes, the stubble on his jaw and—

"I can leave," he murmured. "Even though my sister can be bossy"—a smile—"I'm good at ignoring her."

Sister.

Mahogany hair.

Darker than Scarlett's, but the shades were in the same family, and she could see the resemblance now—in the lines of their noses, their cheeks.

"You really don't smell anything?"

That shouldn't have been the thing she blurted.

But family similarities aside, it was the foremost concern in her mind.

Puzzlement dancing along the lines of his face, but then he shook his head. "No," he said. "Or not anything out of the ordinary. I don't have a strong sense of—"

The door cracked open.

Scar thrust her arm in, holding a can and waving it around until Charlie strode over and took it from her.

Then the door *clicked* closed.

And Charlie glanced down at the can.

Kill her now.

THREE

CHARLIE

It was a deodorizing spray.

A strong one.

Apparently the most powerful one on the market if the label on the can was to be believed.

He glanced up at the petite brunette with the pretty hazel eyes...and the flaming cheeks.

And he got it.

"You smell."

She jerked and promptly winced.

And he felt like an asshole—well, doubly an asshole. First, because he'd made her hurt herself. Second, because he'd just said she smelled.

"Shit," he muttered, striding over to her, can in hand. "I didn't mean it like that. I really...I...um...can't smell you. I mean, I *can* smell things, just not very strongly. My friends always joke that I must have cotton balls shoved up my nose because I can't smell the scent of cherry in the wine we're drinking."

Her eyes, that startling mix of brown and green and gold, met his. "Right."

"So"—he cleared his throat—"in all likelihood, I'm the best person for this job."

Her cheeks flared a little pinker, and he knew that he was fucking this up, but he just didn't know how to make it better. "Right," she whispered again.

"I'm Charlie."

A nod.

"Scarlett's brother."

Another. This one trailed by her hands releasing the costume and going back to her untangling her hair. "Kacee," she murmured.

God. He was such an asshole.

He'd forgotten she was stuck on the costume, forgotten she was in pain.

He moved to her, pressing forward even as she winced back. "I don't smell anything," he said. "I promise."

Her shoulders—or shoulder, since one was still within the suit —lifted, coming up almost to her ear. "I hate my life," she muttered.

"Well," he murmured, trying for gentle and caring and *not* asshole. "We didn't get off to the most auspicious start, did we?"

Kacee's lips parted, surprise darting across her face. "Au-auspicious?"

"Yup." He popped the p at the end. "*Auspicious.*"

"Right," she whispered.

He set the can down, reached for her hair, saw it was tangled around the tab and in the track, so he started untangling it, gently holding the pieces by her scalp and tugging the ends free, a little at a time. She held still, so freaking still that she could have been a statue if not for her chest rising and falling in a steady rhythm.

Too fast to be relaxed.

But she didn't speak as he untangled, and neither did he.

And the silence pressed on him. He wasn't much for waiting people out. He was more of a fill the silence kind of guy. Which was probably why the verbal word slaughter that followed occurred.

"I'm sorry I crashed into you earlier," he murmured.

(That wasn't a terrible start).

But when she just glanced at him, not saying anything, the terrible began.

In the form of verbal diarrhea.

To the most beautiful woman he'd ever seen.

"My ex was in the box next to me. I turned and saw him and freaked out. We were...toxic, and I"—he shortened the truth, omitted that the whirlwind that had begun with a hookup at a conference and had ended with him quitting the company (only to be brought back on and transferred halfway around the world)—"panicked. I ran and then hung out down here because I knew Scar would be around soon, and I just couldn't see Ji-Ho again. Not after what had happened, and—"

"What happened?"

His words stoppered up in his throat for a long second. Then he found them again, right as he untangled the final strands of her hair. "What do you mean?" he asked, gripping the sides of the costume and holding them as she stepped out.

And trying to not be a total sleaze by staring at all that skintight Lycra.

Because it *was* skintight.

And because she had a gorgeous body.

"Why did you two break up?"

"We were..."

"Toxic," she said. "You mentioned that."

"Right." It was his turn to whisper that. "We just...we..." How to encapsulate the drama and jealousy? How to explain that when he'd begun to see Ji-Ho as controlling, he'd stepped back, wanted a break...and then Ji-Ho tried to sabotage his work, tried to get him fired, made his life so fucking terrible that every single day Charlie had gone into the office had felt like torture.

Until the job he'd loved had become a prison sentence.

Until he'd actually thought about ending it all because he couldn't take it.

Until he'd known he had to get the hell out.

Kacee didn't interject when he hesitated—seemingly having no problem with silence or waiting him out. She just remained quiet as he found the rest of his words.

"We made each other miserable."

Her eyes came to his, studying closely, and for the first time, he saw a glimmer of something beneath the panic and avoidance. But all she said was, "Oh."

"Do you want me to step out while you change?" he asked as she moved to a locker in the corner of the room.

"No."

His dick twitched.

Yeah, he was a creep.

But he wouldn't turn down watching her wiggle her way out of that tight Lycra.

Alas, next to the locker was a curtain he hadn't noticed before. She opened the metal door, reached inside, and pulled out a bundle. Then she stepped to the side, tugged the curtain around her.

"You take care of spraying the costume," she said, her voice slightly muffled, and yeah, his mind went straight to her gorgeous body, naked and on display and—

"There's a hook on the far side of the room."

He blinked, torn from the fantasy of what her tits would look like jiggling as she wrestled herself out of those tight leggings.

"You can just hang it there and spray the hell out of it."

She'd have to bend over to tug the leggings off her feet, and then she'd give him a glimpse of her lush ass. She was short, her breasts large enough that they'd overflow his palms, but her ass, those rounded globes would be fucking incredible.

He'd give a lot—a *fucking* lot—to see it in the flesh.

Flesh. Flesh?

Ew.

Enough.

He hung up the costume, popped the lid off the can, and started spraying.

And spraying.

She'd said to spray the hell out of it, so he would do just that. It was the least he could do considering he'd knocked her head off and then said she smelled *then* spent the last few minutes imagining her naked.

So...spraying.

Wielding that can like he was the fucking white knight and she was the giant gold poop-shaped princess he needed to save... from an odor...he couldn't smell.

Fuck.

This was his life, and he couldn't make this shit up.

Coughing drew his focus.

He let his finger off the trigger, glanced over in the direction of the sound, saw that Kacee had her hands clamped over her nose and mouth.

"Too much?"

She nodded, coughed again.

"Sorry," he muttered, capping the can and turning to face her.

And his heart skipped a beat.

He'd thought that she looked gorgeous in leggings and a tight tank top, but Kacee in jeans and a hoodie, her brown hair piled on top of her head took his breath away.

"I think you got it," she murmured, turning for the locker again and pulling out a backpack. He saw what he'd missed before, a strip of dark blue dancing up through her hair, wound into the bun.

"You said to spray the hell out of it," he felt obliged to say.

A glance over her shoulder, the corner of her mouth tipped up. "That I did."

He set the can on the desk. "Well, it's been sprayed."

"Yes, it has." She sneezed.

"And now I've done my best to poison you, as well as knock you unconscious, so mission accomplished."

She snorted. "Don't tell me. You're the assassin Scar hired to take out Goldie so she and PR-Rebecca could have the mascot they've always dreamed of?"

"Yup." A grin.

"But you failed."

"Ah, but have I?" He pretended to reach over his shoulder and withdraw a sword.

She giggled.

And it was the best sound in the world.

It made him feel about ten feet tall. It made him forget that his heart had been stomped on and chucked into a blender for good measure. It made him finally clear that fog from his mind, the shame at his thoughts, his weakness.

"What's next, oh assassin?"

"After swordplay, you mean?"

"Well, obviously."

"Well, clearly, my next ploy is to push you into a lake filled with sharks."

One brown brow lifted. "A *lake* with sharks?"

His lips twitched. "Well, *more* clearly, they're genetically modified sharks that survive in fresh water."

A pause then, "Clearly." She shoved her dirty clothes into a bag, and he didn't miss the fact that it was a zip-top bag—one that she made sure was secure before she shoved it into her backpack. "Will they have laser beams on top of their heads?"

"Why do I feel like the nineties just made a resurgence?"

"Because we're referencing sharks with laser beams?"

He grinned.

She smiled.

And they stood there like idiots...at least until the door opened, Scar poked her head in, and promptly gagged.

Four

S he'd taken a shower that was hot enough to scald off her skin.

Her clothes were on a Tilt-a-Whirl through the sanitary cycle on the washing machine, and she was in front of the mirror, staring at her bare armpits and wondering how in the fuck all her body could produce such a smell.

And how in the hell Charlie couldn't smell it.

She'd studied his face as she'd struggled through the smell that even she could smell (who said her body had to follow the you-can't-smell-yourself rule of biology, because hers certainly didn't and that was how she knew it was B.A.D bad), but he truly didn't seem to be affected by her.

Unless he was an Oscar-worthy actor.

Which, based on her experience with men, was most of them.

Though, he didn't gain anything by lying about her smell. If he was like most men in her life, he would have run at the first glimpse of trouble—or odor, as it were.

He hadn't.

Instead, he'd stared at her like she was beautiful, and he'd gently untangled her hair...and he'd sprayed her suit without gagging. He'd done it *all* without gagging actually.

Because he didn't have a sense of smell.

She giggled.

She couldn't help it.

It was either laugh or cry that *another* person knew her sweat could knock a person dead, so much so that the guys on the team were already giving her a hard time about it.

Hockey gear was notorious for being stinky—or at least at pretty much every rec level, as the NHL and professional teams had people responsible for equipment and keeping that equipment smelling peachy. But apparently it couldn't compare to Goldie.

That wasn't her fault.

It was Goldie's and the fact that the material she was made out of wasn't anywhere near natural. There was no breathing aside from out of two tiny eye holes, so none of the moisture dissipated. Instead, it stayed trapped inside the suit like a humid state. It was Florida. In the middle of summer. With no breeze. Just her breath and her sweat all circling throughout the small space.

A hurricane of stench.

That was her.

But Charlie couldn't smell it.

She nibbled her bottom lip, couldn't resist contorting and bending down to sniff her armpit. Roses and vanilla and bourbon —her favorite scent.

No odor.

Well, okay, there *was* an odor.

But there wasn't The Funk.

And...she really needed to stop obsessing over the smell and Charlie and Goldie. He'd smelled her—or hadn't. The more important part was that he'd helped her. He'd *shared.*

Maybe that was why she couldn't get him out of her head.

Kacee sighed, stopped the sniffing and contorting and got the hell out of her bathroom before she jumped back in the shower and used up all her body wash, until she slapped on several more layers of deodorant.

She was clean.

No more *odeur de funk*.

Just her and her roses and vanilla and bourbon.

Just her and all that...*and* her power tools.

Because nothing brought down her adrenaline high after a game like messing around with some whirling blades. And screws and nails...and the occasional bit of glue, stain, or swipe of a paintbrush. Hinges and decorative hardware. Trim pieces and spending time with her miter saw.

She didn't spend all of her time playing Goldie.

The rest of it she spent with wood...she was *Woody*, one might say.

Oh, man, that was bad.

But this just in, she didn't spend her time being a comedian. In reality, she spent thirty percent of her time inside a smelly costume and seventy percent of her time making cabinets. Big or small. Tall or squat. Painted or stained or distressed. Vanities for bathrooms. Islands for kitchens. China cabinets. Video game storage. Desks and makeup stations and bookcases. She'd even made a sewing chest that expanded out into a large work surface for quilting but could be folded away to look like a simple coffee table.

Simple, creative, a completely new idea that took her hours to design and hours more to build.

She loved making them all.

There was something about the smell of wood in her nose, the feel of sawdust on her skin. The buzz of her saw. The vibration of her sander beneath her palms.

The pride that came from taking something from start to finish, and having clients love it, having them send her pictures of her art in use. She created things that made people's lives better—a little like being Goldie brought a touch of love, humor, and joy to the Gold fans.

Plus, being her alter ego meant that she could afford to make her art.

It wasn't that her cabinets weren't selling. They were, and for increasingly ridiculous prices.

It was that her ex had stolen...*everything*.

Her truck (eventually found in San Jose, stripped of nearly everything that made it a vehicle—engine to seats to radio to tires).

Her tools (and while she'd managed to track down a few of those on Craig's List and Facebook Marketplace, the rest—including the most expensive ones—were long gone).

Her money (from her personal account because he'd somehow figured out her login and had played a shell game of transfer-withdrawal until he'd left her with barely enough to pay her mortgage).

No way to transport her materials, to deliver her cabinets when they were done. No way to make cabinets in the first place.

No—

Nothing.

Starting over.

Again.

God, it sucked.

Living on ramen noodles, working until her fingers bled and her eyes could barely stay open. Taking other jobs so she could pay the mortgage, the electricity, the water.

No Netflix or Hulu. No Discovery+ to get her fill of *Holiday Baking Championship* and *90 Day Fiancé*. No DoorDash or Amazon Prime.

Just...surviving.

She was fucking tired of it.

But she was almost there, almost out of the hole. Nearly at a point where she could start saving again, instead of living paycheck to paycheck. And maybe in a couple of months' time, she'd get her *90 Day Fiancé* back. Kacee had been lucky when the Goldie gig had fallen into her lap. It paid enough that she'd been able to buy a few tools, to keep fulfilling orders, to cover the loss in initial income and keep her in her house—even though her thermostat had firmly stayed in the off position.

But then she hadn't stopped.

Despite the smell.

Because she liked being Goldie.

When she donned that little poop-shaped hat, she could be *anyone*.

Okay, well, she could be *Goldie*. But Goldie wasn't Kacee. She wasn't alone and sad and in a huge financial mess that still had her turning off her water in the shower between shampoo and conditioner and eating half a packet of ramen noodles because she couldn't afford a whole one.

She was a giant poop-shaped triangle of sparkling gold who could dab and twerk and do The Sprinkler, all with equal aplomb.

Carefree.

Not stressed and working fourteen-hour days.

"Soon," she whispered, pushing Charlie out of her head, pushing out Robbie.

It was just going to be her and her wood and making people happy and...maybe she'd be able to make herself happy again someday, too.

She crossed to her closet and moved beyond the pajamas that were calling her name (popcorn, pj's, and poor TV—look, that wasn't the best word for her reality television choices, but she was going for three Ps in that lineup, and on the struggle bus to get there). The point was, instead of those velvet jammies, she moved to her work clothes—a worn flannel, thick old jeans that protected her thighs and knees—and quickly donned them.

She had a couple of sketches to complete, several cabinet doors to fit.

And maybe she'd go a little further and build some drawers while she was still riding that post-game high, set the top. Her current client wasn't pushy in the least, but she knew they were anxious for the combination bookshelf-changing table that would be taking up nearly one wall of their soon-to-be-filled nursery.

Mom—Savannah—wanted to nest.

Dad—Tim—wanted Savannah to be happy.

And Kacee was in that place in a project, slightly more than halfway, screaming for her to just put her head down and *Finish. This. Shit.*

Plus, finished meant money, and she sure as shit needed *that*.

Then she could move on to the next shiny thing, or required thing, or...whatever was going to get her out of this mess *thing*.

Then maybe...maybe someday soon, she might be able to have something she wanted.

Something that wasn't just ramen.

FIVE

CHARLIE

He walked into the office and was greeted with a feeling of dread.

One he hadn't had in a few months.

And one that was solely due to the man standing by his desk.

Fuck. He didn't want to deal with this. Not now. Not *ever* again.

Charlie turned on his heel, decided that he needed a cup of coffee. Not because he thought that he could use it as an avoidance technique, but because he thought that he needed caffeine to deal with what was going to happen.

Not a scene.

Ji-Ho didn't make scenes.

He was quiet like a viper.

And no surprise, he struck before Charlie had even managed a sip of that liquid caffeine.

"Baby."

Charlie's fingers tightened on the handle of his mug. Not because of the endearment, or maybe it was. Maybe it was because he would have given anything to hear that soft tone a few months ago, when everything was bad and he'd wanted things to work out so desperately that he'd been willing to do almost anything.

But he was done with that.

So the *baby* just left him feeling sick.

"Hi, Ji-Ho," he said, spinning around and taking a sip of his coffee. "It's good to see you, but I have work to do. Maybe we'll catch up some other time."

Like never.

Never catching up.

Never having a conversation that wasn't work-related.

Never hearing him say *baby* in a way that made an oily feeling slither down his spine.

Fingers gripped his arm, digging in fiercely. "You don't get to—"

The door to the break room opened, and Kelsey strode in. Her eyes widened, gaze going from him to Ji-Ho before dropping to Ji-Ho's fingers on his arm.

"Hi," she said softly, glancing up at Charlie for a long moment before heading over to the counter and picking up an apple.

"Like I said"—Charlie deliberately tugged himself free of Ji-Ho's grip—"we'll catch up some other time."

Ji-Ho's dark brown eyes flashed, but he didn't say anything further to argue, probably because Kels was carefully washing her apple, slicing it into pieces that a chef would be proud of. Then he huffed out a breath and left.

Charlie waited a moment before he let out *his* breath.

"You okay?" Kels asked. "That seemed...tense."

Another inhale. Another quiet exhale before he took a sip of coffee. "I'm good," he said, turning toward her as she arranged her apple slices on a plate and added a scoop of peanut butter.

She dropped the spoon into the sink, snagged the plate, and stared at him. "Yeah?"

He made sure that his next breath—or sigh, really—was silent. "Yeah," he said.

"Right." She picked up an apple slice, dipped it in the peanut butter. "Well, if you're ever *not* good, just let me know, okay?"

A smile—forced, yes, but it was there. "Of course," he agreed, sipping as he spun toward the door, not able to stop his shoulders from slumping with relief when Ji-Ho was nowhere in sight.

―――――

"No. *No!*" they shouted when the characters—or reality TV stars (or, really, same difference)—on the television embraced...or rather kissed and groped and then disappeared behind a bush to consummate their short-lived love affair that was so short-lived, it probably wouldn't last beyond the island.

"Good God," Fanny said, as the camera zoomed in for a close-up before cutting to black, "that was a *lot* of tongue."

"Too much tongue," Charlie agreed, shuddering. "*Way* too much tongue."

"And it cost the group, what? Five? Six K?"

"At least," he agreed, shoveling popcorn into his mouth. It paired perfectly with the chardonnay that he'd picked up from the winery Fanny and her husband, Brandon, had gotten married at. A winery they visited frequently, and one that he and Fanny had gone to the previous weekend, ostensibly to see the local sights, but, in reality, to stock up on wine for reality show nights.

The timer dinged, and he set the glass and bowl of popcorn aside.

"Pause the show," he ordered. "I need to check on the lasagna."

Fanny stuck out her bottom lip but dutifully paused the show, picking up their glasses and carrying them both into the kitchen for a refill.

"If that pouty lip is because I didn't make ravioli, then tuck that away, missy," he said. "You know Scar would flay me alive if I made that when she wasn't here."

"Well, then she shouldn't be stealing my husband in the process."

"You mean that Kaydon shouldn't be off doing his job—one he can do really well in part because you helped him come back after his injury—with my sister and your friend tagging along because she's doing *her* job? And *your* husband on that same trip because he's doing *his* job by negotiating some contracts for Kaydon while they're in Boston?"

She made a face. "Don't be logical."

Since the pan was full of bubbling goodness and crispy cheese, he pulled out the pan of lasagna and set it on the counter. Then shoved in the sheet pan loaded with bread sliced half open and topped with tons of butter and garlic.

He set the timer—because if he didn't, he always burned the bread.

"Then don't be a pouty baby," he said. "And tell me about the new skating program." She had stuck out her bottom lip—like the pouty baby she was being—but it went away when he brought up skating. Because she loved being on the ice, loved teaching kids, and loved helping athletes reach their full potential through her skating school.

"Well, the summer clinics went so well," she said, "that I have a few private sessions scheduled over the All-Star break, and those are going to pay for the scholarship program I want to start."

He nudged her. "You know you can get Scar to put together a fundraiser for you to add to that."

She shuddered. "I still have repressed trauma from the last one."

"I don't know that it's *very* repressed."

Considering she'd married the man who'd won after being raffled off as a prize.

A swat to Charlie's shoulder, but then she moved by him for the wine bottle and topped off both their glasses. "Trust me, whatever you see on the surface is backed up by a shit-ton more beneath it."

"Is this where I remind you that Brandon won your raffle prize...which then won *you* a husband."

She glared. "Not the point, butthead."

"*So* the point," he teased, dodging the dish towel she'd scooped up and tossed at him, then moving to get the plates ready.

A little salad because they had to pretend to be healthy.

Silverware because they weren't monsters eating with their hands—unless it was popcorn or garlic bread or the cookies he'd made for later.

Okay, they *might* be monsters, or at least those who ate with their hands.

But they weren't monster enough to eat *lasagna* with their hands.

Or *he* wasn't anyway. Who knew what petite, little delicate Fanny might do with a bottle of wine in her?

(Probably the type of monster who would still eat her lasagna with a fork).

Anyway, he digressed.

They had carbs and cheese ahead of them, three more episodes of their new favorite reality show, and a night with his friend.

No Ji-Ho.

No tension that had crept into his frame every morning he'd walked into the office that week, expecting his ex to show up again.

No sick feeling in the pit of his stomach as he waited to be cornered or hissed at.

He could just hang out with Fanny. They could be their normal goofy selves, and he didn't have to think about the past or the future.

Just that moment.

Just...finding a slice of happy when it seemed that he was only destined for sad.

Because when he hopped out of the Lyft that evening, pleasantly buzzed and stumbling up his walkway, gaze glued onto the front door like it would tractor beam his ass into his house, he missed that Ji-Ho was standing on his porch.

Six

KACEE

"It's amazing," Savannah murmured, running her hand over the pale gray painted top. Kacee had scribed that part of the changing table so the pad wouldn't slip off. Trying to think about all the ways this would be used now and in the future, making it as functional as possible.

That's why she had also included soft-close drawers—so little fingers wouldn't get pinched—adjustable shelves so they could be brought up or down depending on the size of the books their kiddo would be reading—picture to chapter. And knobs that could be reversed if the little boy they were having wasn't feeling the sparkling, crystal pulls that currently adorned the drawers.

"Thank you," Tim murmured, shaking her hand. "This is more than we could have ever expected."

"I'm glad you guys like it," she said, stooping to pick up the blanket she'd had wrapped around the piece when she and her assistant, Jimmy (paid fifty bucks cash for helping her schlepp all of her deliveries) had carried the changing table up the stairs.

He was waiting in her rental truck—because she hadn't saved up enough to buy a new one yet—so she really needed to get him back to his wife and kids. His wife, Maddy, had been cooking dinner when Kacee had swung by to grab Jimmy, and the smell of whatever she had in the oven had made Kacee's stomach rumble. Jimmy needed to eat that while it was hot, and maybe, if she looked pathetic and/or hungry enough, she could bum a plate before she returned the rental.

Right on cue, Tim passed her over a check and they chit-chatted as he walked her out, Savannah murmured a distracted goodbye, her hand on her rounded belly as she opened and closed the drawers.

The front door clicked closed behind her as she hustled down the walk and hopped into the driver's seat.

"All good?" Jimmy asked.

She nodded, turned on the engine, pulling out of the driveway and taking him back to his place. It didn't take long, maybe twenty minutes, but he spent the time catching her up on his kids—eight- and six-year-old girls who killed it on the soccer field and whose American Girl doll obsession he fueled by doing these deliveries with her.

Then they were sliding to a stop in front of his house and he was hopping out of the passenger's seat, starting to slam the door.

"Wait," she said, reaching into her pocket and pulling out his cash.

Jimmy grinned. "LoLo would kill me if I forgot. It's her turn."

Kacee grinned back. "New doll or accessories this time?"

"Oh, accessories all the way, baby." A chuckle. "Apparently it's the number one rule for all women everywhere. Her rule," he added, waving a hand at his hoodie and jeans, "clearly not mine."

Laughter bubbled up in her chest and she mirrored him, waving a hand down at her own clothes. "Well, clearly that's not my rule either," she said. "But glad to help her with her accessorizing."

He grinned. "By the way, Kace, you build damned good cabinets. Just so you know."

Warmth in her chest, spreading out, filling her up.

Compliments...she wasn't used to them.

"And you schlepp them *damned good*." She nodded to the house. "Now get on inside. Your girls are waiting."

He tilted his head toward the front door. "Did you want to come in and eat with us?"

Yes.

Yes, she fucking did.

But she also didn't want to intrude, and if nothing else, she hated feeling like a fifth wheel. Which was the only reason she said, "Oh, no, I couldn't possibly put you guys out like—"

"Kacee Jane! You get your behind inside my house and at my table right now!"

Jimmy grinned again. "I think you've been summoned."

She sure had.

Her eyes flicked to the truck's clock, mentally calculated how long it would take to eat, play with the girls, and get back across town to drop it off in time.

She did that mental calculating fast because...she'd already been calculating on the way back to Jimmy's place. Hell, she'd pretty much been calculating from the moment she'd smelled whatever Maddy was cooking just over an hour before.

"I guess I can't ignore that, can I?" she asked, turning off the ignition and hopping out.

"Not if you want to live," Jimmy teased, leading her up the walkway and in through the door. Immediately, LoLo and Carrie were there, calling out her name and wrapping their arms tightly around her waist. Fluffy, their three-pound (maybe, if she were rounding up) Chihuahua hopping up on her back legs and bouncing in time to her little yaps.

It was chaos.

It was beautiful.

"Hi, girls," she said, hugging them back before glancing up at Maddy, "What can I do to help?"

Maddy lifted a brow. "Wash up and get your butt in a chair, missy. I've been waiting for you two to pull up so we can eat."

Kacee's heart squeezed. "You shouldn't have."

Maddy huffed and flicked her towel in the direction of the kitchen sink, not bothering to answer that. "Sit," she ordered after Kacee had joined the kids in washing her hands, pulling a tray of sliced potato wedges out of the oven.

That smelled...like fucking heaven.

Yes. Absolutely divine.

Potatoes were cheap, right? She could probably afford some potatoes the next time she went shopping. Did they sell potatoes at the dollar store? *That* she wasn't so sure of. Maybe she could get some on sale at the grocery store, but then again, she wouldn't have the spices or the butter or oil. She'd used the last of anything good several months before. Would they taste okay if she crumpled up a bay leaf?

No.

People didn't eat bay leaves.

Maybe she could boil them in some water *with* bay leaves. Maybe that would do something and—

"Ms. Kacee! Come sit by me!" LoLo yelled, patting the chair next to her.

"No, *me!*" Carrie yelled, somehow even louder, but then again, she had two years on her sister, so maybe she had more lung strength?

Either way, it snapped her out of her mental rabbit hole about bay leaves and potatoes (not before she came to the conclusion that, no, boiling potatoes in water with bay leaves that were approximately a century old wouldn't make up for not having butter or fresh herbs...or some real talent in the kitchen).

She was okay.

But she wasn't *Iron Chef* or *Chopped* level.

She wasn't taking random ingredients and turning them into something gourmet.

She was...boiling water and hoping all the salt in her body

from the bouillon didn't make her blood pressure go through the roof.

"How about," she said, moving toward the girls and pushing all thoughts of potatoes out of her head, "I sit here." She tugged out a chair at the head of the table, gestured to it. "LoLo sits *there*." Then she pointed to the chair on her right. "And because Carrie and I are both lefties, Carrie sits here." A nod at a chair on her left, paired with plunking down at the head of the table, taking Jimmy's spot, but knowing he wouldn't care if it meant preventing a fight between the girls.

Kacee hadn't been over loads of times, but she had been over more than enough to know that once they got going on the fight train, it was hard to stop them from chugging right along that track for the rest of the meal.

In the sense of world—and parental—peace she prayed to the Sibling Gods that her attempt at distraction would work.

LoLo and Carrie studied each other.

LoLo stuck out her bottom lip.

Carrie decided things when she sat in the chair Kacee had indicated and said, "Lefties are the best!"

LoLo's bottom lip slid out further. "Nah-uh!"

"Lefties and righties are both perfectly awesome," Kacee interjected. "Now, when's your next soccer game, Lols? I want to come."

Her eyes lit up. "Really?"

"Really," she said.

"It's next Sunday and we're..." She went on to describe the team she was playing, apparently for some regional championship thing, which seemed altogether too serious for a bunch of six-year-olds playing bunch ball, but what did Kacee know about kids and sports?

Other than that, these girls were all in, competitive as hell, and their parents supported them.

So...regional championships. Next Sunday. Four o'clock. Leaving her enough time for a full workday.

"What about my game?" Carrie asked. "My team is playing, too!"

"I'd love to watch you, too." She leaned back as Maddy set a plate laden with food in front of her. "When is it?"

"You'll regret asking," Maddy muttered, turning back to the counter and retrieving more plates.

Before she could ask why, Carrie clued her in. Or partially, anyway.

"It's at eight on Sunday."

"At night?" That seemed awfully late for a school night.

"Oh no," Maddy said. "It's at eight in the *morning*, Kacee. And an hour away."

The garbled sound she made was a mix of horror and sympathy. Horror because getting up early because she'd be in her garage working until she was exhausted...aka working until the wee hours of the morning was going to be brutal. Sympathy because Jimmy and Maddy did this regularly.

Big brown eyes on hers. "Are you still going to come?"

The Puss-in-Boots wide eyes that could convince her to do *anything*. Hell, who was she kidding, she would have agreed, even without the sad puppy eyes.

"Of course I am," she said. "And I'll even bring donuts."

"Really?" Carrie asked.

"Really."

"What are you bringing to mine, Kacee?" LoLo asked.

Fuck. She'd already been calculating the cost of those donuts and how two dozen of them would keep her in ramen for a month.

But wide brown eyes, expectant smiles. Two girls relying on her.

Young, innocent, sweet, competitive, amazing girls.

"Oh, no, Kacee doesn't have to bring anything," Jimmy began.

"I'll bring donuts, too," she said. Because...in for a penny, in for a pound. "If it's okay with your parents," she added, not wanting to cause trouble for them.

It came anyway, she supposed.

Because those wide, hopeful eyes turned to Jimmy. "Is it okay, Dad?" they asked in unison.

He shot her a look that said *he* knew at least some of what she'd been going through, even though she tried to hide it behind smiles and talk of everything being totally fine, *pretending* everything was fine. He knew she was hurting, but she also knew that he didn't know how much she truly *was* hurting, otherwise he wouldn't have accepted her money.

But he needed that, too.

Not that the girls expressly *needed* American Dolls. But they were six and eight and were so innocent and bright. They needed to know they could get a silly cell phone for a doll or a new dress or a stethoscope.

They needed to not worry about all the things she'd worried about growing up.

They *needed* to live in a world where life was soccer and dolls and meatloaf and a family friend bringing donuts to their soccer game.

Later, the world would intrude, try to make them small and stamp out the spark inside them. Later, they'd have to fight to stay strong, to build their lives, to hold on to that fire inside.

So now, *now* it could be about them.

"It's okay," he said after locking eyes with Maddy for a moment.

"That's settled," Maddy said, sitting next to Jimmy and picking up her fork. "Donuts and early morning soccer." She shot Kacee a small smile. "So now let's eat before Kacee runs screaming out of the madhouse that's our life."

"What's a madhouse?" LoLo.

"Why would she run screaming?" Carrie with furrowed brows.

"I like running." A beat before Kacee added, "And screaming."

Maddy's small smile grew and Kacee grinned back.

Then she got to eating.

———

She juggled her backpack and the bag of leftovers Maddy sent home with her and sighed when she spotted what Jimmy had done.

Or rather, what he'd left when he'd walked her out to the truck.

The fifty dollars she'd given him were shoved into the cupholder.

Glaring at it, knowing that she wasn't going to leave it there, she scooped it up, shoved it into her pocket, and then checked the inside of the rental for any other rogue belongings. Even though she knew that she wouldn't find any.

No surprise, she didn't.

So, she slammed the door, shoved the keys in the drop box, and then shrugged on her backpack. Two and a half miles to her house. It wasn't a long walk. But it was autumn with the first tinges of winter, and her hoodie wasn't going to cut it. She'd have to remember that for next time. Heavier coat, maybe a few more layers, a beanie.

At least her belly was full.

That meatloaf was the shit, and she had another plate of it, one that she'd make sure would last her a few days, even if she wanted to open the plastic container and down the potato wedges that Maddy had packed her.

She wouldn't, of course.

Just fantasizing about stuffing her face with them would have to be enough.

"Discovery+," she whispered. "I'm doing this so I can get Discovery+."

And a truck. And keep her house. And be able to afford to heat it.

But she was focusing on the small things. On the five dollars a month she would be able to afford once she'd bought her truck and could take on more clients when she didn't have to worry about paying a rental car fee or owing someone a favor for borrowing theirs when she took on large jobs again. On the donuts she couldn't afford to buy for the girls...but that she could now that she had her fifty dollars back.

On the fact that she was slowly crawling her way out of her hole.

On the two and a half miles she needed to walk in order to get home.

Right.

She'd better get moving or she would never get her ass out of this cold.

Focus on her surroundings because it was dark and cold and she was a woman walking alone at night. Focus on summoning warmth into her hands and fingers, as though thinking it and moving fast enough might mean that she wouldn't be cold.

Focus on...her projects.

Her newest baby that she had spent hours sanding the night before, turning the wood buttery soft, brushing away the sawdust, knowing that the desk was going to be one of her favorite pieces yet.

Sometimes she felt like a foster parent, collecting her babies and sad to let them go.

Well, not like any foster parent she'd grown up with. They'd been happy to collect the check and kick her out that front door. There were good people doing good work in the system...she just hadn't experienced them.

So maybe, she felt like the cat lady she followed on Instagram, the one who took in kittens to senior cats, and who cried when she had to let them go. Even though she knew she had to, that they were going to good homes, that without them moving on, she wouldn't have space to help others.

That was what she felt like when she turned her cabinets loose in the wild.

Would they oil the butcher block she'd so carefully crafted as often as they should?

Would they be gentle on the hinges and use a soft cloth to clean the doors?

Would they partake in coaster-usage?

She hoped they would, but she also couldn't sneak into their houses with her chamois cloth and buff up their cabinet fronts.

The light in the crosswalk turned and she headed into the residential neighborhood where her house was located. Mature trees, wide sidewalks, quiet streets. It was peaceful and so much more than she could have ever hoped to own.

That peace, walking along the nearly silent sidewalk a couple of blocks from her house, was part of why she'd fought so hard to keep her house.

Even though the mortgage nearly killed her every month.

She just needed to get her truck, and then she could take on more jobs.

And she was close to that.

Just a couple more months and she'd finally be making progress.

And then a few more and she would have her Discovery+ again.

So close she could almost taste it—or watch it, she supposed.

Kacee paused as a car passed in front of her then turned right onto her court, passing a house with a giant blow-up black cat, spiderwebs hung over the bushes, and orange lights wrapped around the porch railing. Another had a plethora of gray foam coffins pressed into its lawn. Two doors down from that, there was a pumpkin that played thunderstorm sounds and set off a cascade of flashing lights.

Her house was at the end of the court, at the top of the cul-de-sac. She had a couple of plastic pumpkins on her front porch, and her banister on the porch was wrapped with sparkling purple and silver garland she'd gotten on sale a few years back (and it turned out that her ex didn't think holiday decorations were worth stealing). So she might not have flashing lights and thunderstorm sounds, might not have fresh pumpkins, but she didn't let down the neighborhood.

And now she was just realizing that she needed to budget for Halloween candy.

Because her neighborhood got a shit-ton of trick-or-treaters.

So, maybe like a few more months plus a couple more before she got her binge on.

But worth it, because the kids deserved a good night.

Plus, it would be the best entertainment she'd had in ages—a parade of Thors and Elsas and the odd kid dressed up in something homemade and awesome.

She took a few more steps and was maybe ten houses away from her place when she heard it.

A hiss of sound.

One heartbeat of it and she knew—*knew*—what it was.

It sent prickles down her spine, had her feet skittering to a stop on the sidewalk. Once it would have sent her skittering into the shadows.

Now, it meant that she did something.

Pulling out her phone, just in case, she moved up the walkway...and she saw *him*.

In the arms of a beautiful Asian man.

A beautiful man with high cheekbones, kissable lips, and hair just long enough that one lock fell over his forehead and screamed for someone to lean close and push it back.

And he was holding...Charlie.

Close. In an embrace that normally would have sent her walking the other direction.

But she'd heard that hiss, and that meant she looked closer, *saw* what was happening.

The ex.

This must be the *ex*.

Charlie was trying to put some distance between them, his head turned away, his body language screaming that this wasn't welcome, but he also didn't know how the fuck to get out of it.

God, did that call to her.

It had her feet moving faster, had her shoving herself in between their bodies, had her wrapping her arms around Charlie's shoulders and...

Kissing him.

SEVEN

CHARLIE

One second, he was tipsily trying to extract himself from Ji-Ho's grip, his mind racing and surprise and wine making him slow as Ji-Ho hissed insults at him.

The next, he had a woman pressed against him, her mouth on his.

A soft floral scent, breasts against his chest, gentle lips slanted across his.

"Hey, baby," she said, pulling back slightly—

She said.

She.

Her.

Kacee.

What. The. Hell?

"Sorry, I'm late." She tilted her head toward his front door, completely ignoring Ji-Ho. "Should we go inside?"

He heard his ex suck in a breath, probably ready to hurl another insult, and rage sank straight into his bones, burning deep through the marrow. The surprise faded. Rage intruded, and his hands that had somehow gone to Kacee's waist fisted, resting against her hips.

His jaw clenched.

"You—" Ji-Ho began, eyes flashing, looking almost black in the dim light.

But Kacee was already moving and doing it in a way that dislodged Ji-Ho's fingers—and not a moment too soon because Charlie had been ready to pull back his fist from her waist, and cold-cock the fucker.

Fucker.

Not his ex.

But the *fucker*.

He let that settle deep inside him, but only for a second because Kacee's fingers wrapped with his, and she tugged him forward, drawing him up the steps onto the porch. "I'm tired, baby," she said, pitching her voice so that Ji-Ho couldn't help but hear her, even though she didn't once look at him or acknowledge him. Instead, those fingers stayed tightly wrapped around Charlie's. "Let's go to bed."

Charlie glanced back, saw that Ji-Ho's face hadn't softened, but there was confusion in his eyes, enough that he wasn't saying anything as Kacee reached into his pocket and pulled out his keys, unlocking the front door, and leaving Ji-Ho standing there staring after them, shock written all over his face.

But he only saw it for a second because then Kacee was shutting the door, flicking the lock, and tugging him farther into the house.

She moved with a purpose, as though she'd been there dozens of times before, drawing him into the kitchen and flicking on the light...and then going to the window over the sink and glancing sideways out the glass. "He's gone," she murmured after a moment. "His car just pulled away from the curb."

Charlie paused.

Less tipsy, still surprised.

Really freaking on his back foot.

"I...um...what are you doing here?"

She'd just turned back from the window, and he watched as her cheeks flushed bright pink. "I'll go as soon as I'm sure he's not coming back," she said softly. "I"—white teeth nibbling into a plump bottom lip—"live down at the end of the court. Next to the Fosters."

The Fosters were old busybodies, and Mal cut his grass with precision using his lawn mower, weed whacker, and, yes, a pair of scissors for those pesky stray blades that didn't fall in line. Susan was...Christmas cookies and knitted scarves. They were rigid and nosy, but surprisingly cool, hosting bi-monthly barbecues and dropping off baskets of homemade preserves—yes *preserves*—on neighborhood porches.

He also knew the house next to theirs.

The one with the wraparound porch and the woman who never came to the barbecues, mostly because she was working all the time—or at least that was his intel from Mal.

Silence had fallen while that slid through his mind.

And then awkwardness crept in.

Because what in the fuck all kind of man was he that this woman, tiny, curvy, with a face like a fucking angel, had to save *him* from his ex?

He was supposed to be riding in on a white stallion, shining up his armor. He was supposed to save the day and make it count and...

He'd stopped doing all the things he was *supposed* to do years ago.

Couldn't say that it didn't sting, though. He hated that Kacee had seen him like that. Hated he was so fucked up from the breakup, from Ji-Ho being in California that he was off his game and couldn't just tell his ex to leave.

Why had he just stood there, fucking empty inside, unable to do *anything?*

"I'll...um..." She hitched a finger over her shoulder. "I'll just go."

In this instance, with the reality of her leaving, he managed to unfreeze, to move toward her. Not touching her. They'd kissed—or really, she'd kissed him to break the tension of that situation—but he didn't think she would invite that kind of contact. Not with the way her gaze was sliding away, her steps sliding back to the hall.

"Wait," he whispered. "Don't go. I just—"

She adjusted the straps on her backpack, on the one he just noticed she was wearing. "I should let you get on with your night."

"Why did you—" He shook his head. "*How* did you—?"

"I've"—those eyes, warm now, returned to his—"been there is all. I heard it, and I just knew."

More silence.

Then she cleared her throat. "I need to go."

Right.

Of course she did. She was trying to go about her evening, hadn't planned on being his white knight.

"Let me walk you home," he said.

"Oh, you don't have—"

"Let me rephrase that." He leaned in, held her gaze, finally shrugging off the fog and the confusion and the *hurt*. "I'm walking you home."

Wide eyes.

Another readjustment of that backpack.

One that had something in him snapping—ice, maybe—a frost that had surrounded him for far too long, dulling every thought, muting every sensation, knotting his insides until he was a tangled ball of anxiety that was barely functioning. The world came flaring back into him, breaking that ice, flinging it away in a shower of shards that was more dramatic than any scene from a Hollywood movie.

He stepped forward, tugged the bag from her shoulders, slung it on one of his own.

Then he walked to the front door.

Opened it.

And began walking to her house.

Knowing that she would follow.

She did.

———

She paused with one hand on the knob, the other extended, held out for her backpack.

He moved up to her, pushed open the door.

Then when she didn't move, he all but invited himself inside and stepped beyond her into the hall, flicking on the lights, since they were in the same exact spot as his place.

But her place was nothing like his.

For one, his had furniture.

Hers was...not empty, exactly, because there was a sad-looking loveseat set along one wall and a blocky wooden table in front of it. There was a mount for a TV on the opposite wall. No pictures or artwork, no knickknacks on the built-in shelves.

"I'll take that," she said quickly, grabbing the straps and trying to tug the bag out of his grip. "Thanks for carrying it in."

"You just move in?" he asked, eyes trying to process as he turned slowly, his gaze going to the kitchen.

"What?"

"Did you just move in?" he asked again, and when her brows furrowed, he added, "I'm happy to carry boxes, and I'm damned good at organizing a kitchen if you need help."

More furrowing, her lids blinking slowly.

Then her expression shut down. It didn't make sense, because she actually smiled at him. But that smile—and her eyes—went empty. "Oh, yeah. I...um...moved in...a bit ago. Been busy with" —she cleared her throat—"work. Well, work has been really busy."

"Being Goldie?"

"Oh, no. Goldie is just for fun." A flicker in her gaze he

couldn't discern, because it was there and gone in a flash. "I'm a woodworker."

That surprised him.

That...stalled him.

Because he didn't know what a woodworker did.

She smiled then, a real one this time. "Don't know what that is, do you?"

"I mean..." he said. "In theory, I know what a woodworker does." He leaned back against the wall, crossed his arms. "Clearly, you work...wood."

Kacee snorted.

His cheeks heated as he realized what he'd said. "Not *that* wood," he hurried to add. "Wood from trees and um..."

She giggled, shook her head, and set her backpack on the ground. "Come on," she said. "It's just easier if I show you." Her ponytail fanned out when she spun on a heel and moved to a door on the other side of the fridge, the one in his house that led to the garage.

And when he followed her, he saw that it did.

Her garage wasn't like his.

It didn't house a car.

It contained...well, it looked like *This Old House* had exploded.

A workbench took up the majority of the far wall—filled with organized cubbies and shelves, shiny, pristine tools, perfectly painted wood. The center of the space had several works in progress. One cabinet with gleaming mahogany stain sitting on a pallet. Another one that looked like it was part skeleton—or at least bone-like with slender pieces of wood pointing up to the ceiling. There was another, a desk, he realized, and this workspace was well-used and covered with smudges of paint and stain and stacks of papers.

Kacee moved toward it, and he started when she shoved it back, realizing that the whole unit was on wheels.

That explained the smudges.

They were fingerprints.

"That," she said, "is an armoire." She nodded at the stained chest standing on the pallet as she picked up a piece of paper, showing him a sketch that shocked him in its realism. It was identical to what she'd built, albeit in much smaller scale.

"That's amazing." He held the paper gently, walked to the armoire and circled it, taking in the details, the craftsmanship. It was beautiful, and he'd seen enough furniture to understand that she was incredibly talented. Charlie started to extend a hand, stopped before he touched it, unsure if the stain was dry, especially since the smell of the lacquer was strong in the air (and if he could smell it then it must be *really* strong). "Can I touch it?" he asked.

A widening of her eyes, as though she was shocked that he'd even want to.

But then she nodded and he kept reaching, fingers grasping the edge of the drawer, drawing it open.

"That's not a dovetail joint," he said, smoothing his hand over the wood that had been sanded until it felt like butter.

More widening. "Um...no," she sputtered, "it's something I came up with. A combination of a dovetail and a tortoise."

He didn't know what that latter was. Pretty much the collective knowledge he possessed had been used in knowing the way the pieces of the drawer were joined together wasn't a dovetail joint.

So yeah, he was impressed that she'd come up with her own way.

Impressed by the entire space, her work—almost done, just begun, the drawings.

"What's that one?" he asked.

Her throat worked, and she gently took the paper back, walking to the desk and picking up another from the pile.

She handed it to him.

And his mouth fell open.

"You can build this?"

It was a mid-century modern piece, so different from the armoire that it almost made his head spin. The armoire was heavy, ornate. Beautifully built, yes. But totally different from the clean, boxy lines of the TV stand.

He found himself drawn to the desk, to the pile of drawings.

A changing table. Bookcases. Tables. Chairs. Kitchen cabinets. A closet system. A murphy bed. More bookcases. More kitchens. Vanities for bathrooms. Built-in organization systems and family room cabinets and a door that he realized he'd seen before.

"This is Kaydon's," he murmured.

She frowned, glanced at the drawing. "How'd—" Then, "Scarlett," she said softly.

"Yeah," he said. "It's beautiful. Did you do the shelves inside, too?"

A nod. "All the wood in that room. The paneling, the window frames, and the door. The bases and crown." Her lips twitched. "I did pretty much everything except putting the books on the shelves."

"Considering the amount of them, that might have taken you longer than the actual door and shelf-building."

Now she smiled, and it was a beautiful thing. "You're right."

He flipped through a few more drawings, loving this insight into her, loving the soft but confident way she showed off her work.

But as much as he wanted to dive deep, to learn more, to *see* more, to be in her presence—gentle and easy and *warm*—she was wavering on her feet, and she stifled a yawn.

"I should go," he said.

"Do you want a beer?" she asked.

He should let her go to sleep.

But he didn't want to leave her. Not yet.

"Sure, honey," he murmured. "Thank you."

"Right." A nod. She spun on her heel, led him out of the garage.

He paused to carefully set down the stack of drawings then followed her, stepping into the kitchen, just in time to get a glance at her fridge.

Her *empty* fridge.

Not even the usual stockpile of condiments and old salad dressings.

He frowned.

Pink on her cheeks. "Or...um..." She cleared her throat. "I forgot I haven't gone shopping yet. Can I get you a glass of water?" She moved to a cupboard, opened the door, revealing a mostly empty interior.

He'd take a glass of pretty much anything from her.

But the bright lights of the kitchen highlighted something else.

The dark circles under her eyes.

"I should let you get some rest," he said gently. "It's late, and if I'm remembering the schedule correctly, don't you have Goldie duty tomorrow night?"

A sudden stillness through her body, her movements almost wooden when she closed the cabinet door. "Yeah," she whispered. "You should go. It's late. And I do have Goldie time tomorrow."

Silence.

Then, "Thanks for bringing me home."

He stepped toward her, curling his palm around the side of her neck, his thumb brushing over the delicate skin where shoulder met throat. "Thanks for rescuing me from my ex."

"Are you—?" She nibbled her bottom lip for a moment. "Are you okay?"

"With my ex showing up at my house and acting like the asshole he is?" Charlie laughed darkly. "No, I'm definitely not. I've made it clear that we're done, moved halfway around the world to get away from him, and...he's back."

"I'm guessing it's not a romantic gesture."

"I don't know *what* it is." And he didn't really know how to feel. It wasn't romantic. He didn't want to go back to the toxic that was his relationship with Ji-Ho. He was *done*. But he also didn't have the same...vitriol that Ji-Ho seemed to have.

Why did he hate him? Why did he have to keep pushing, keep spewing?

Why couldn't Ji-Ho just let it go?

Charlie thought that he knew, or at least partly. Ji-Ho was competitive, brutal, aggressive. Serious alpha vibes to his own beta ones.

But most of all?

He didn't like to lose.

Not a deal. Not a fucking game of Bananagrams.

And definitely not a relationship—or at least not one that he didn't end himself.

Charlie had ended things.

That didn't fit into Ji-Ho's plan.

The toxic turned into obsession turned into...following him halfway around the world.

"Just...not something you want."

Not phrased as a question, but the question was present anyway.

"No," he murmured. "No, I don't want it. We're not—won't ever be. We were a possibility, something that had moments of good, but we were two people who brought out the worst in each other." He shook his head. "I'm sorry. I'm probably rambling and not making any sense."

A beat of quiet, her hip leaning against the island. "It makes perfect sense."

His brows lifted.

She answered the unasked question. "My ex and I were our own brand of toxic." She tucked back a strand of her hair, giving him a flash of that strip of blue. "Looking back, I almost don't know the person I was when I was with him."

"Man, do I know *that.*"

A ghost of a smile.

He wanted to know more. He wanted to talk and move closer,

to hold and kiss and feel the silk of her hair on his skin again. But those dark circles ate at him, as did her next smothered yawn.

"Sleep," he murmured.

She seemed to feel the same way. Her body drifted closer. "Overrated—"

Then she yawned again, and this time it wouldn't be smothered.

It was loud and long, and her cheeks were flushed pink afterward.

"Sleep," he repeated.

That pink didn't fade. "Right," she whispered.

With reluctance, he dropped his hand, stepped away from her. "You'll lock up when I leave?"

A nod as she walked into the hallway, moved to the door, and held it open for him.

"Kacee?" he asked when he paused on the porch.

"Yeah?"

"Can I buy you dinner after your Goldie time tomorrow?"

Not the smoothest line in the least.

But that warmth in her pretty hazel eyes grew.

Then dimmed, pink growing.

"I—"

"After I bring you back here to shower," he said quickly. "And I'll spell Scar so I can be on spray duty again and she won't be such a drama queen."

"It's not drama," she muttered. "It's bad, and I don't think that normal guys are supposed to ask stinky girls out."

"I'm not a normal guy."

A beat. "No," she whispered. "No, I don't think you are."

He let the silence linger, then murmured, "I'll pick you up at five tomorrow? Drive you to the game?"

More silence lingering.

This time from her.

His heart started pounding.

She was going to say no.

He knew it. He knew—

A nod. "Okay."

"Okay," he repeated, and then he touched his mouth to hers, forced himself to not deepen the kiss, to say goodnight and walk down the stairs, pausing only to order her to lock up.

He hauled ass out of there before she could change her mind.

It didn't hit him until he was walking back down the sidewalk to his place that those shelves and cubbies, hooks and drawers hadn't been created in a day. That had been months...*years* of work. It didn't hit him until then that he hadn't seen any moving boxes. He spun, glanced back to her house, saw the driveway was empty, as was the curb.

She could have been like him, had a few too many and gotten a ride share home.

But...no furniture.

No knickknacks or art.

No TV.

An old loveseat and an empty fridge and a crudely built coffee table when she had a workspace filled with magic.

No jackets on the hooks lining the hallway.

Two glasses in the cabinet.

A couple of bowls and a short stack of plates.

No, she hadn't just moved in.

No fucking way.

And he knew, *knew* with some instinct deep in his gut, that it had to do with her ex.

And he knew—*knew*—that he was going to find a way to fix it.

Eight

She'd let him in.

She'd let him see too much.

And now she was going on a date with him.

A gorgeous, smart man who seemed interested in her. *Her*. Asking her questions about the construction of drawers of all things.

Dovetail?

And making jokes about spraying her down and Scar being a drama queen.

Dinner.

With her.

What. The. Fuck?

She looked around her kitchen, at the cabinets that were gorgeous but empty, knew that the rest of her house was the same.

No belongings cluttering up the shelves.

No art on the walls.

Clothes in the closet that could be crammed into one duffle bag.

Her life had shrunk...no it had always been small. She'd always been ready to pack up and leave at a moment's notice.

Lie.

For a few years, she'd believed it could be more.

Her tools couldn't fit into a bag. The paintings that had once hung on the walls weren't expensive, but they *had* been special. The frames Robbie had taken (and the photographs he'd left behind) equally so. His clothes in the closet. His deodorant on the counter, toothbrush in the holder. His jackets on the hooks she'd hung on the hall.

That had all been special.

Because she'd let him in.

Been vulnerable and raw and told him everything.

And he'd left.

He'd known every dark thing and secret and all the memories that had caused her pain, that still woke her sometimes with nightmares. He'd held her and told her he would always be there to carry them away, to make it so they couldn't touch her.

And. He'd. Left.

Charlie would do the same.

She knew it. He'd hold her in strong arms if she let him, would show empathy, interest, maybe even slay a demon or two.

But eventually he would leave.

Probably without her tools and her TV.

But even that she couldn't know for sure.

She couldn't know *anything* for sure...anything except that she had to prepare for the eventuality when he would go.

Which meant she had to break off the date.

It would be stupid to put herself into that position.

Except...

Bright blue sky-colored eyes. Deep red stubble on his jaw. Lips that she wanted to taste.

"Why can't I just have one date?" she whispered, running her fingers over the woodgrain. "Just one and be done."

A taste.

Enough to fill her up, to savor, to hold her over.

And then it would be done.

Why not? What would it hurt? she thought.

Of course, this was the moment she should have known, should have realized that it would hurt.

Because, for Kacee, it *always* did.

———

He was waiting for her outside her changing room, a can of deodorizing spray in hand and a sexy smile on his lips.

"Thought I'd avoid the concussion," he murmured, stepping close and tugging off the top of Goldie's head.

Before she could tell him that she didn't like to remove the top without being safely ensconced in the room (no magic of characters would be ruined for children on *her* watch), Charlie was ushering her into her little changing area and closing the door. Goldie's head went where it belonged—on the top shelf of the storage locker—thus proving that he paid attention.

But she knew that already, didn't she?

Dovetail drawers.

Fingers drifting across sanded wood.

Focusing on her, on her drawings.

She sucked in a breath—

Which was seriously the wrong thing to do.

Her nose burned, and she immediately gagged.

Charlie just smiled and held up the can, lips twitching when he declared, "I'm ready." And seriously, how was he so caviler when she was dying of embarrassment? This was twice now that the most gorgeous man she'd ever had the privilege to lay eyes on was spending his time deodorizing her.

Because she smelled.

Horrible enough to make her own eyes water.

He set the can on the corner of the desk and moved toward her. "Arm up," he ordered, reaching for the zipper. Undressing her...if stripping her out of a smelly gold turd could be considered undressing.

But then the zipper was down, his palm was cupping the back of her head as he lifted the costume over the top of her, freeing the top half of her body, sweat making her black tank top she wore beneath it cling to her skin.

He knelt in front of her.

She shivered.

"Sorry," he murmured. "I know it's probably cold. I'll hurry."

Cold was the least of what she felt, not that she told him that. Not when his hands were on her hips and he was kneeling in front of her. Not when his assuming that position meant that she had all but swallowed her tongue, moisture flooding between her thighs. It would be *so easy* for him to peel down her leggings, to spread her thighs and bury his mouth in her pussy.

And God, it had been so long since a man had his tongue on her body, his lips on her skin, and sometimes even his teeth. *Please*, let him not be averse to teeth. A nip, a small bite of pain was sometimes the best sensation in the world. It ramped desire, sent her hurtling toward or over the edge...especially when it was soothed by a flick of the tongue, a press of the lips, a kiss that was long and deep and...not on her mouth.

His hands slid along the outsides of her legs, drawing the rest of Goldie down her body.

It should have been uncomfortable, this man touching her. He was practically a stranger.

Except...he wasn't.

Well, he was, of course. But he wasn't. And no, she couldn't explain that, same as she couldn't explain why she had agreed to the date in the first place, why she hadn't canceled it after she'd come to her senses.

There was something drawing them together.

And she was there for it.

Soaking it up, holding it tight.

For the moment.

Because it *would* be fleeting.

But at that moment, with a leanly muscled, sexy man kneeling in front of her, his hands shaping her curves, and she was hot, absolutely burning up, literally in that there was sweat dripping down between her breasts, but figuratively as well, desire pulsing through her in a steady thrum that had her hands trembling.

"Here," he murmured, his voice with the slightest bit of rasp that had a quiver sliding through her middle. "Lean on me."

When she didn't move, he took her hand and placed it on his shoulder

Then his hand was wrapping around the back of her calf as he lifted one foot and then the other, drawing the costume off and setting it to the side. Goldie was a mass of lumpy, shining gold fabric, and she wasn't pretty.

But the way that Charlie was staring up at her made her feel like she was.

Finger by finger, his hand slid from her skin, or her leg anyway. But she *felt* it on her skin, right through her leggings, as though it had been imprinted on her limb.

"You want me to step out while you change?"

She blinked.

And it took her way too long to answer the husky question.

"Or are you comfortable behind the curtain again?"

Another

Then it processed.

God, he was such a good guy.

Another reason why she'd agreed to dinner.

Because there weren't too many of them. Because once it was over between them, she would remember that.

Because once he left—and he would leave—that might be all she had to hold on to.

Tools aside.

She could always hold on to those.

Except when they were stolen.

Except when she was losing her mind thinking in circles.

Except when he was staring at her expectantly. Patiently, but expectantly.

Because...right. She was supposed to be answering that question.

"You can stay," she whispered.

His hand came to rest on her ankle, stroking his thumb lightly over the tiny gap of exposed skin between her sock and the bottom of her sweats.

Stroke. Stroke.

"Okay, sweetheart," he murmured.

Stroke. Stroke.

And she was wet. Just like that.

Another reason she'd agreed to the dinner. Because of the pull she felt when he was near. Sparks in her veins, tingling in her fingertips, heat in her center—

More expectant looking.

Right. She needed to go about that changing.

She shifted—just slightly, just barely adjusted her weight so that it was more on her heels than her toes—and like he noticed everything about her, he immediately released her, standing so their chests were aligned, so their bodies were close.

His head dropped.

She inhaled.

Fingers on her cheek, lips close...

And then he stepped away.

She swallowed hard, pulse pounding in her veins, and then she managed to get her legs working and walked across the room to the locker, luckily remembering that step two after step one of changing out of her sweaty clothes was to put on new, fresh, *non*-sweaty clothes (though, if she wasn't smelly and stinky and needing that shower, she might forgo the clothes and pull back the curtain and see what happened).

Or maybe...

If she was going down with Charlie Andrews, she wanted to crash and burn.

"Charlie?" she asked after she'd wrestled her way out of her leggings, top, and sports bra...and after the copious amount of spraying had cut off.

"Yeah, sweetheart?"

Her heart pulsed.

She liked that.

Liked *sweetheart.* Liked the soft way he said it. Liked how it made her feel.

Her fingers gripped the side of the curtain.

His voice came nearer. "Kacee? You okay?"

She was naked. Slightly sweaty. No doubt stinky, though the funk was sort of contained in the giant Ziplock she'd shoved her clothes into.

But...

She was *naked*.

And he was interested. And she wanted him. And she was going for it. And—

She pulled back the curtain.

His mouth dropped open, but only for a moment. Then his eyes heated, he took a step toward her, and—

The door to her changing room flew open.

NINE

"Oh my God!" Scar exclaimed. "You're totally hired for spray duty."

The door slammed against the wall, making him jump.

He caught one glimpse of Kacee's horrified face—after he'd managed to pry his gaze from her dusky nipples, her hips that screamed for him to grab on tight, heft her up, and have his way with her...okay, have *many* ways with her.

From behind with that heart-shaped ass jiggling—also thank God for her whirling around and giving him a peek at it before she remembered to flick the curtain shut.

Against the wall, her legs around his hips, her breasts flush to his chest.

On top, so he'd see them hanging down in front of him, so he could lean up and suck her nipples deeply into his mouth, feeling the hardened beads against his tongue.

"Charlie?" Scar asked, her brows tugging together.

The curtain was closed, but he was lost in his own head, his own fucking fantasies—literally *fucking* fantasies—and he didn't realize that Scar had come all the way into the room, that the door was now closed, that she was staring at him with concern, clearly expecting a witty comment, or at the very least some sort of response to her comment.

"Sorry," he said, holding up the can. "I think I got high there for a second."

She giggled. "I know the feeling." Then she held up a bag and called, "Oh, Kacee, dear *Kacee*. Whenever you're decent, come out. I have a present for you!"

Silence. Then—and he could hear the embarrassment in her tone, though it appeared that Scar, his lovely, usually very perceptive sister, couldn't. "Just a second," Kacee said quietly.

Or if Scar did sense it, she didn't acknowledge it.

Or put it together. Thankfully.

Despite Kacee agreeing to dinner, she was still as skittish as a racehorse. He could feel it, feel that she was on a razor wire, waiting, just waiting for something to tip one way or the other. He didn't know what those ways were yet.

But he was going to find out.

And he didn't need the collective of the Gold and their various back-office staff intervening, no matter how well-meaning their intentions might be.

"Scar," he began. "She's changing and—"

The curtain pulled back. This time not revealing the image that would be forever imprinted on his brain—the best image of his life, frankly, and he'd thought Ji-Ho had the sexiest body he'd ever seen.

Hard, crisp lines.

Soft, lush curves.

They were both intoxicating.

But there was something about Kacee that called to him, that made those curves even more alluring. A vulnerability. A strength. Inner cracks that he wanted to patch over.

And boy, that should have his alarm bells ringing.

Especially, since he'd been *all* about plastering over those inner cracks of Ji-Ho's.

Let me fix you, broken, gorgeous sexy man with the slice of inner blackness. I—and only I—can do it!

But the cruelty that had always been present in Ji-Ho's personality—the cutting comments phrased as jokes or constructive criticism, or—hello, gaslighting—as Charlie *misunderstanding* or *taking everything too personally* or *cultural differences, so you need to toughen up*—that cruelty wasn't present in Kacee.

She barely knew him and had intervened in a tense situation —and something that could have potentially blown up into something serious or violent or dangerous (and now he was realizing he needed to talk to her about that because she shouldn't be walking into situations like that).

The point was that the inner cracks in her hid kindness.

And he had to protect that kindness, that good, that...essence that made her *her*, especially if it had her building such beauty in her garage, smiling so sweetly, offering him a glass of water when her cupboards were bare.

So, when Scar seemed to not notice that vulnerability and uncertainty, he opened his mouth to intervene.

A hell of a lot less serious of a scenario than a confrontational ex.

But when Scar got something in her mind, she could be just as dangerous...albeit in completely different ways.

The curtain slid back, revealing Kacee in a hoodie, her hair piled on top of her head, a pair of jeans that hugged her thighs to ankle and disappeared into a set of clunky boots with bright red laces.

"Pressie time," Scar declared, skipping over to Kacee—and fuck, his sister was cute. It made his heart feel like it was filled with helium and rainbows and puppies and cotton candy to see that. To see she was happy and fulfilled and had a man who loved her exactly as she deserved.

Loved her too much, sometimes, he thought, wrinkling his nose and smothering the protective instinct when he noticed the slightest bit of stubble burn on her throat.

And thought about all the surfaces he'd taken to disinfecting when he'd been staying in Kaydon's spare room before he'd moved out and begun renting this house.

Now they were living at Scar's house. For the moment anyway.

She and Kaydon were taking a few months to live together in each house before deciding whether to sell her place or Kay's.

Kay's was objectively nicer and more luxurious.

But Scar's had sentimental value, both because she'd worked her ass off on it and because the team had banded together to surprise her with some finished rooms a few months back.

She'd used part of the money Heath had left them to buy the fixer-upper.

Her half of the life insurance policy they hadn't known existed. Her half that their parents had been after—well, truthfully, they had wanted *both* of their halves—but Scar had given them half of her half and because of that, their parents had wanted more.

Always, they wanted more.

Charlie had refused them.

They didn't get him, didn't understand his sexuality, his personality, how he would never be the same as their god-like eldest son, Heath.

Who was dead now.

Sick for too fucking long. Then eventually gone—and in a way, it had been a relief because he was out of pain, but mostly it had hurt.

Because the Three Musketeers had become two.

Another reason it had been easy to move to Korea. Because the connection was broken, because Heath had given him the means to go. But even though he regretted that he left Scar to their parents and her grief, felt sharp stabs of guilt when he thought about leaving her alone, part of him would always be glad he'd gotten away.

Of course, that time away had imploded into something that left scars on top of scars.

But he was stronger now.

Broken and reformed and all the wiser for it.

And now standing in the same room as a woman who made his heart sing.

She reached a hand up, fussing for a moment with the messy bun on top of her head before Scar all but shoved the present into her chest, forcing her to drop her hand to her front, to grab the bag before it hit the ground.

Her eyes drifted to his for a moment—and only a moment because Scar was practically vibrating with excitement, her red hair shimmering like a cape where it laid in long, shining waves down her back—then, probably to put his sister out of her misery, she tore the tissue paper out of the little gold bag (black paper, because Scar loved a theme and knew how to make things look good).

Then she pulled out...a key.

With a little Goldie-shaped keychain.

"New swag in the store," Scar said, still vibrating, though a grin had joined the party.

Kacee smiled, her face softening. "It's adorable."

"Agreed," Scar said. "And joining the party of stuffies, sweat-shirts, socks, and even picture frames to show off all those Goldie pictures."

"Wow."

"You're a celebrity."

Kacee wrinkled her nose. "A stinky celebrity who nobody knows her face."

"Objectively the best kind," Scar quipped.

Kacee, her eyes dancing, turned the smile to Charlie. And he felt the impact of it in his soul, tapdancing along his spine, spinning pirouettes in his gut, launching itself into the air only to land softly on the balls of its feet in his lungs.

And his heart...it simply reached out and grabbed on tight. Gripping fiercely, squeezing and digging its nails in.

Not letting go.

Not when he wanted to make it his life's mission to see that smile again.

"Did you see what was on the end of it?"

He snapped out of his revelry in time to see Kacee frown at Scar. "What do you mean?" she asked.

"Well," Scar reached out and tapped the keychain. "I gave you *that*, but you didn't ask what the key went to."

A tiny frown between Kacee's eyes, her gaze going to her hands, presumably to the key hanging off one corner of Goldie's poop-shaped body.

"It's to your own locker room!" Scar burst out.

Loudly.

Making Kacee jump.

Making Charlie somehow love his sister even more.

"Come on," she said, taking Kacee's hand and drawing her into the hall. Charlie followed at a more sedate pace, watching his sister drag the woman he was rapidly deciding was his (how caveman of him) down the hall.

Two, three, four doors down.

Then drawing her to a stop.

A flourish of her hand, a goofy bow—God, his sister was a dork—and then the door was open and Scar was basically shoving Kacee inside.

Since he was practicing sedateness, he arrived a few moments after Scar and Kacee.

Which meant that he focused on Kacee rather than the surroundings when his gaze hit the room. She'd gone ramrod stiff, her throat working in a way that looked absolutely painful.

"What is this?" she whispered.

That was when he looked away from her and began focusing on the surroundings. A shower stall in the back corner, a changing stall on one wall, similar to the one that guys had in their locker room (the private one for showering, with cubbies and hooks and a lockbox for valuables, not the public one where the media were welcome). Taking up most of the opposite wall were two more Goldie costumes, and the final corner, tucked almost behind the door, was a huge bag-like thing, surrounding a pole and a hook and—

Honestly, he didn't know what the hell that was.

Scar put him out of his misery—or his confusion anyway.

"It's to fumigate the costumes," she said. "That and with the other two in rotation, and we hope that you won't have to deal with Stinky Goldie."

"I—"

"Oh!" Scar said, skipping over to the shower. "And so you don't have to go home feeling stinky."

"I—"

This time Kacee wasn't cut off. Her words faltered on her own, feet carrying her across the room, stopping at the bench and picking up something.

Black undergarments branded with the Gold logo, he realized.

Her lips parted. Her throat worked again.

Scar noticed what she was holding. "So you don't have to ruin your own clothes. Oh, hold that thought," she added, hustling out of the room.

Kacee was quiet.

Too quiet, something was wrong that tugged at his heart, and he took a step toward her, determined to find out what when Scar hustled back into the room, Goldie in tow. "Watch. Watch how quick this works. You can hang your undergarments in here on one side, Goldie on the other"—she hung both up, only gagging the slightest bit—"zip it closed, and hit this button." She did as described, and the machine whirred to life. "Either that or you can leave it for the equipment guys. Richie said he's happy to manage her."

"I—"

Scar stopped talking, probably waiting for Kacee to find the words.

He knew he was.

But when the silence stretched, Kacee's throat still working, her gaze on Goldie and the whirring zipped-up bag, Scar seemed to get that she was overwhelmed and gently put her out of her misery. "Now, you'll be stuck going to dinner with us," she teased lightly. "Because I won't be over-dramatically gagging in the corner and making you lose your appetite."

"I don't know what to say."

At least it was a full sentence.

"You don't have to say anything," Scar told her, moving toward Kacee and squeezing her hand. "I know you don't think it's a big deal, but you get the crowd going, and the guys feel that on the bench. That helps them play better, not to mention the front office loves the social media presence, and before you tell me, it's not because of the costume. It's the energy that you bring to her. The joy and smiles and laughter."

A shrug. "I'm just dancing and giving away some T-shirts."

Scar slung an arm around her shoulders. "You think you're just giving away a few shirts or pucks or snapping some pictures, but you're important, Kacee. You're a part of this team—you're family."

More throat-working.

Scar's voice grew soft. "And I know I'm new to the team, to the Gold family myself, but you belong here, too, Kacee. And we're not letting you go."

Silence.

Tears glistening in her eyes. "I'm not used to having a family," she murmured after a moment, slicing into his heart with the truth laced through those words. "And I didn't need a shower or more Goldies."

"I know," Scar said. "But we wanted to give you them, so shut up and deal with it."

Kacee jerked, eyes going wide.

Scar flicked a hand back, tossing her hair. "Yup. I said that, and I meant it. You're family, so you're gonna have to just get used to it."

A quiet moment, the air tense. "So, you're saying the team is like the mafia," she murmured, and Charlie's heart jumpstarted at the light humor. "Once you're in, there's no getting out?"

Scar nibbled at her bottom lip. "Well, I didn't say *that*."

"Don't listen to her."

They turned, saw Kaydon leaning against the doorframe, smile on his lips, warmth in his eyes. "She's saying *exactly* that." He came into the room, patted Kacee on the shoulder before winding an arm around Scar's waist and tugging her back against his chest. "You're in and stuck with us, and there's no way that you're getting away from us now."

Scar made a face. "I am not..." she kept talking, but Charlie wasn't listening.

Nor when Kayden quipped something back.

Because Kacee's eyes had dropped, and he knew she was looking at the same thing that he was when he saw longing cross her face, felt that same yearning in his soul.

That strong arm.

The closeness.

The way that Scar immediately relaxed against Kay's chest. How he hardly seemed to notice that he was tracing his palm up and down her arm.

It was instinctual. *Real.* And so damned rare and valuable that he couldn't help but want some of that of his own.

Which was probably why he did what he did next.

Why his feet led him across the room and into Kacee's space, his own arm curling around her shoulders, drawing her in, pressing her front to his side. Her hair grazed his jaw and felt like silk. Her body was tense for only a heartbeat before it melted.

Just *melted*.

Right.

Complete rightness soaking into every cell.

He was soaking that in, which was why it took him way too long to process that his sister and Kaydon had stopped bantering.

The room was silent.

And he'd just declared his intent, his interest, his *need* for Kacee in front of his sister...and one of the Gold's biggest gossips.

Ten

KACEE

She stared at the menu, trying to push Scar's gleeful expression out of her mind, and wondering how underdressed she was for the restaurant Charlie had taken her to.

Okay, not so much underdressed as underclassed.

Plenty of other people were in jeans and hoodies.

Her date outfit, nicer jeans with a blouse she'd picked up from the secondhand store, the one she'd spent far too long trying to figure out, was still lying on her bed.

Because she'd showered in her new changing room.

Hot water she didn't have to pay for.

Clothes she could put on again because she hadn't spent too long in them, and her special brand of *odeur de* Goldie hadn't had the opportunity to permeate.

Because although Charlie had offered to drive her back to her place and wait while she changed, she hadn't wanted to inconvenience him. Not even when she was struggling not to hyperventilate in the shower his sister had arranged for her, one that was nicer than her own (and had exceptional water pressure and a better showerhead). One she didn't feel guilty for using for long minutes.

Because of that hot water she didn't need to pay for.

But the guilt came for other reasons.

Worry about how much money Scar had spent on her—she'd finished the shower and headed into the hall, heard Scar mention to Charlie that it came out of the maintenance budget. Would there be enough left for all the things the team needed? A shower for a smelly mascot seemed to be far down on the priority list.

What if the team didn't get what they needed and it was because of her?

What if—

"We can go somewhere else if you want."

Charlie's voice had her head jerking up.

When her eyes hit his, he nodded at the menu she was holding in her hands. Holding because she certainly wasn't reading it. More like letting the words swim before her eyes as she fretted.

Yup.

Fretted.

About her upcoming broken heart.

About the money spent on her changing room.

About the gift that had been in the bag, the one she hadn't noticed, wrapped carefully in tissue paper, that was from the guys. They'd each thrown in a couple of bucks and had gotten her some expensive shampoo and body wash and a loofa.

And a hairbrush that was many steps up from her dollar store special at her place.

Hell, *all* of it was many steps up from her dollar store specials.

And the budget and the fact that Charlie had waited in the hall while she cleaned up, chatting with Kaydon and Scar and Brit and Coop and Calle, so that when she'd come out (after using the blow dryer that had been kindly stowed under the little vanity that sat next to the shower stall), she'd had the full Gold experience.

Meaning inquisitive eyes.

Nosy questions before Charlie had shepherded her away from the crew.

Gentle teasing called down that hall.

Which meant they all knew about her and Charlie, and so they would all know when she ended up broken-hearted...and they all would probably take his side when he was done and—

Warm hands on hers. "Breathe, sweetheart." A squeeze and she was staring into the bright blue of the summer sky again, lost in that cloudless atmosphere and utterly entranced by the sunbeams, the warmth, the gentleness.

A balmy breeze on her cheeks.

The kiss of summer on her lips.

And no time at all to focus on the fact that the man had seen her naked.

Oh. God.

This man had seen her naked.

Naked.

And she was just going on with her day like it was no big deal to be sitting across a table from a man who'd seen her naked not even two hours before, who she would have fucked *at work* if not for the fact that *his sister* had walked in on them.

"Oh, my fucking God," she whispered.

"That's not breathing, sweetheart."

It wasn't. Unless one exhalation of air that was accompanied by words could be considered breathing.

Because she wasn't inhaling. Nor was she exhaling again—with or without words.

Her lungs were frozen and black spots were encroaching on the edges of her vision.

A swipe of his thumb across her lips, pulling the top from where it was melded to the bottom, allowing air in. His other hand slid to her shoulder, massaging gently, grazing the front of her throat and finally, *finally* she sucked in a breath.

"S-sorry," she whispered on the next one. "I—I—haven't had—"

"Shh." A gentle admonishment. "You don't need to explain yourself to me. I've had panic attacks before."

He *had?*

A nod, even though she knew she hadn't spoken aloud.

"And I know it's not super helpful to tell you to breathe," he said gently. "I always hated it when people told me that."

She did, too.

Hated it so much.

She was trying to breathe, of course she was. But it was like her body had a mind of its own, and it just wouldn't let her get enough air into her lungs.

Except with Charlie.

He'd stopped it.

"It was your touch."

Confusion written across the bright blue sky.

"Your touch grounded me."

Even as the sweat she hadn't realized had beaded on her forehead, gathered on the backs of her knees, in her armpits (and God help her, why the fuck was she always sweating around this man?) began to dry, she knew that the contact had pulled her out.

A gentle thumb on her lips, her skin.

Soft words—even with the dreaded order to breathe—had helped.

But mostly, it was just Charlie.

Because he felt like her safe landing in the stormy sea. An anchor, a pier, something to tie herself to, for however long it took for the storm to pass.

His fingers slid from her skin, dropping to her hands again, but not until she felt more centered. And how the fuck he knew exactly when that was shouldn't have surprised her—the man's timing was impeccable, and he seemed to notice everything about her, focused on her in a way that no one had ever—ever!—before. "We can really go to another restaurant," he said. "If this is triggering you."

"I—" For a moment, she was out of words.

Again.

Then annoyance bubbled up and she powered through. "It's not the restaurant," she blurted. "It's because you saw me naked."

Stunned silence.

After a long moment, his lips curved up at the corners. Slowly. Sexily. So much of the latter that her uterus contracted and moisture gathered between her legs.

"It was a fucking gorgeous view, honey."

Now that moisture was growing, gathering at the tops of her thighs.

"Well—" She cleared her throat, chin coming up, heat glazing the tops of her cheekbones. "I mean, it wasn't just that. I was overwhelmed by what Scarlett did. That was really nice and too much and—"

"It wasn't."

She frowned. "What?"

"It wasn't too much."

"I—uh—I—" Another cough, trying to free the words—or maybe her brain had slid out of her soul and lodged itself there because this man turned the organ to mush. "I'm not used to that."

A statement that revealed too much.

She knew that the moment the words crossed her tongue.

Charlie paid attention. He was observant, and that statement was like waving a red flag in front of a protective, manly man. His fingers convulsed on hers. His eyes were suddenly clouded with thunderstorms.

"I know, sweetheart."

"I didn't mean—"

"And you'd better believe that I'm going to be the man who's going to change that for you."

Her throat spasmed.

Fingers on her jaw, his face coming close to hers. "You deserve the world."

Pulse pounding, she tried desperately to say something, to say anything. But what did a woman say to that?

"And I'm going to give it to you."

She choked.

———

"I'll take the…" Her gaze scoured the menu, reminded her why she'd felt like such a fish out of water before the panic and the thinking about the fact that he'd seen her in all of her nakedness and the whole *I'm-going-to-give-you-the-world* thing.

Reminded her because everything was *expensive*.

Really freaking expensive.

Who paid twenty-five dollars for a salad?

A *salad!*

Salad wasn't even a good entree. Who liked all that slimy green stuff as an actual meal (okay, so she liked a salad for the main course every once in a while, and it actually sounded good since she'd been surviving on instant ramen for months, because something green and healthy might not be the *worst* thing…except for the whole *twenty-five dollars* thing!)?

The point was, the salad was the cheapest thing on the menu.

And it was twenty-five dollars.

And God, *one* meal at twenty-five dollars.

She couldn't remember the last time she'd been in a position to spend that on one meal. Not when every five, ten, twenty dollars went toward her mortgage, toward replenishing her tools, toward crawling herself out of the hole that her ex had left her in.

"I can come back if you need more time," said the waiter, an attractive male with an unfortunate handlebar mustache (curled up at the edges—ick—though the non-judgy part of her reminded her that she firmly ascribed to the *you-do-you* mentality…even when it came to handlebar mustaches).

"No," Kacee hurried to say. "I'll take the…" Her gaze dipped to the sides. Nine dollars each. Still a lot, but she could work with that. "...the potato soup, please."

"And for your main?" he asked.

Fuck.

"I'm actually fine with just soup," she began.

The waiter's brows knitted together, but his lips curved up into a smile that was polished and professional. "And to drink?"

"Just water is fine."

A slightly deeper V between his eyebrows, but he nodded, turned toward Charlie. "And for you?"

"The tomahawk steak," he said, glancing at her, "medium, okay?"

"I—"

"We're sharing," he told the waiter. "Medium. Two sides of Brussel sprouts, a baked potato loaded, a side of the garlic fries, the mandarin orange salad, and a bottle of the..." He named some wine that was probably expensive off a menu she hadn't bothered to read. "That okay with you?"

She nodded mutely.

First, she didn't know what it was.

Second, he'd just ordered an insane amount of food.

The waiter's face had relaxed, and he smiled widely (probably thinking of the twenty-percent tip on an insanely expensive bill that would soon be coming his way, because she knew—*knew!*— Charlie would be a good tipper). "I'll bring out the soup and salad first." A chuckle. "Well, the *wine* first, and then the apps."

"That's perfect," Charlie said. "Thanks."

The waiter disappeared, the sky landed on her, a thunderstorm in the distance. "Want to tell me why you ordered the single most least expensive thing on the menu?"

Her throat seized up.

And she squeaked.

Squeaked.

Dear lord.

His hand found hers again, held tightly—not painfully—but

not gently, either. Just in a way that she knew she wouldn't be able to escape. Not now. Not ever.

A thought that sent her pulse pounding.

She wanted to be ensnared.

She was desperate to be free.

ELEVEN

CHARLIE

Her eyes came to his, and the sane part of his brain told him to lay off.

To not push.

To back off and let her tell him in her own time.

But...he couldn't stop himself from pushing, just a little bit.

Not when she was so thin and her cabinets were bare and the fridge was empty and she acted like Scar setting up a changing room for her was the nicest thing anyone had ever done for her. Not when she apparently wasn't used to people thinking about her, considering her, looking out for her.

That pissed him off.

"I'm not very hungry," she squeaked.

Her cheeks were pink. Her gaze fixed firmly over his left shoulder.

And...her stomach rumbled.

Loudly.

Those cheeks went fire engine red. He raised a brow. "Right."

Silence fell between them.

This time he waited, not saying anything further, clinging to his patience...and was rewarded. "That salad you ordered was twenty-five dollars. That steak"—she choked—"I don't even want to know how much it was. My eyes just kind of glazed over when it reached the meat section."

When she left that as though it were answer enough, he asked, "So you decided to get soup?"

"It was safe. And cheap." Her voice dropped, as though she were surprised she was sharing what she was sharing. "And if you decided the date didn't go well and needed me to pay my fair share, then I could afford soup." Her eyes hit his. "I can't afford paying half of a soup and salad and wine and steak and Brussel sprouts and a loaded potato."

A whispered admission.

One that sent an arrow thunking into his heart.

"In what world would you think that I would ask you out on a date and then expect you to pay?"

Hazel eyes darkening. Her lips pressing flat. "In *my* world."

Another whisper. Another admission that sent a flurry of arrows into his heart. Tearing him open, bleeding him dry, sending rage boiling through him. For the world she thought she lived in, the one that hadn't been kind to her.

The one she'd given up on.

The one that he was going to raze to the ground.

He squeezed her hand, drawing her eyes back to his. "Well, in my world, I don't ask the person I'm interested in out for a meal and expect her to pay. And I sure as shit don't take her out for dinner and have her leaving hungry." He laced his fingers with hers. "So, we're going eat salad and steak and loaded baked potatoes. We're going to stuff ourselves and then walk out of here with leftovers that you're going to take home and have tomorrow. Because we're not paying eighty-nine dollars for a steak and leaving a single bit of it for them to throw away—"

"Eighty-nine *dollars*?" she gasped.

Her lips formed a tiny O.

Her eyes had gone wide.

And he had to kiss her.

Had to.

So he did, leaning across the table, trapping their interlaced hands between their chests. A brush of his lips to hers.

And he was lost.

This was different from before, from outside his house. It wasn't a surprised kiss—at least not on his part. It wasn't a sneak attack or a surprise.

It was...perfection.

That pulse in his heart, that tiny hook dug into him, attached to an invisible line that slowly, inexorably reeled him in, burned this moment into his mind, onto his soul.

She made a soft sound at the back of her throat—a moan that had his cock hardening, one he wanted to hear every day for the rest of his life—then her lips parted and her tongue slid into his mouth.

The edge of the table dug into his gut. His back started aching from the contorting he was doing to keep his mouth on hers.

And he didn't give a fuck.

He'd break his spine if it meant that he could continue kissing this woman.

She tasted like cherries. Her tongue was a sleek, hot dart as it danced with his, meeting him touch for touch. *No.* Not meeting him.

Leading him.

Stoking the flames of desire between them, making him forget about the clank of plates and silverware, the hum of conversation surrounding them. Reducing the world into just the two of them. Their lips and tongues and mouth. Their fingers interlaced, pressed between them. His heart pounding against his rib cage. His cock rigid in his pants, insistent against his zipper. Heat flowing through him, making every inch of his skin tingle.

A throat clearing.

He heard it distantly. Mostly because he was focused on the kiss, on the feel of Kacee's skin beneath the fingertips of his free hand which had drifted to her shoulder, dipping into the neckline of her T-shirt.

Then he heard it again.

Dropped back into himself with an abrupt crash—the sensations cutting off, the noise intruding, reality snapping him back into focus.

He pulled back, but not very far, still holding her hand, gripping her shoulder, the molten silk of her skin beneath his fingertips. Her lips were swollen. Her pupils dilated. He wished for once that his sense of smell wasn't so dulled. He would give a lot to have the scent of her in his nose, to inhale her deep into his lungs and keep her there. To have the full effect of her rather than the faint sense of female and sexy woman and something sweet like fruit—would it be cherry like her lip gloss?

Or maybe something floral? Rose or lilac or jasmine.

Instead, he had to soak in the bit of her, hold it close like it was the most precious gift in the universe.

"I'll just pour this—"

He blinked, tearing his gaze from Kacee's face and focusing on the waiter, whose cheeks were slightly pink and eyes were fixed on the bottle of wine, on the two glasses he was pouring.

Charlie managed to sit back fully, leaving their fingers linked, extending his arm across the table in order to do so. It wasn't remotely comfortable, but she was hanging onto him just as tightly. So, he wouldn't let her go.

The waiter slid the glasses over, depositing one in front of each of them.

Still not looking at them.

Still with red on his cheeks (note: don't kiss Kacee in public for fear of being arrested for public indecency and/or embarrassing their waiter so much that he was ready to make a run for it...whoops).

"I'll just go check on those appetizers."

Then he was gone.

And Charlie couldn't summon an apology. Especially not

when Kacee glanced up at him as he pushed her glass a little closer, picked up his and took a sip. Her mouth curved. Her eyes twinkled, and she asked with a hint of pride, "I guess I'm drinking the wine along with your tongue?"

So not what he expected her to say.

Which was probably why he choked on *his* tongue.

Then burst out laughing.

Looking proud of herself, she swirled her glass, bent and inhaled deeply, then drank.

———

After the wine and kissing and the laughter, Kacee relaxed.

Probably because conversation had drifted to the team, and it was an easy topic to discuss. How the team was doing. What she did when she was being a mascot.

He loved the way she lit up when he asked her about the T-shirt contest from during the game, how she'd been able to list the names of the kids she'd interacted with during the intermission entertainment on the ice (helping the littlest boy, apparently named Matthew, win the tricycle race by cutting the corners— *cough,* cheating—so he crossed the finish line first).

Then he managed to get her talking about her cabinets.

Which was like sticking a key into a lock and opening up her soul.

She'd described her current projects, chattered about her new scribe saw (whatever that was, because it had been a hell of a long time since he'd watched episodes of *This Old House* with Heath, and despite his pulling out dovetail on that first night, his long-term memory reserves were all but depleted).

But she hadn't been a selfish talker and had asked him loads of questions about himself and his work.

Which he found significantly less interesting than hearing her talk about herself.

Still, he knew it meant something to her when he shared, too, knew it when her fingers convulsed when he shared about his current work project. He was working with Kelsey Scott and she was absolutely brilliant. While it might not seem exciting to be streamlining a few things on the back end, stuff that no users would actually see, he was excited that the process would be cleaner.

Nothing like efficient code and a positive experience for the people maintaining it.

So, the conversation had been enthusiastic and positive and completely without drama or heavy and dark.

Plenty of time for that in the future.

Now they had pulled up to her driveway.

Her empty driveway, and he couldn't say that the dark intruded, exactly. But reality definitely did. He liked being with Kacee. She was beautiful and kind and smart. She was also wounded and tentative and maybe a little bit broken inside.

Then there was the empty driveway. The empty house. The empty cabinets and fridge. Her worry over the twenty-five-dollar salad and ordering the cheapest thing off the menu.

She worked two jobs.

He knew those cabinets were expensive, just as he knew that while the mascot job didn't pay a mint, he did know she shouldn't be struggling and worried like she was.

So, what else didn't he understand?

Why was she working so hard and seemingly not having much to show for it?

A house.

Tools.

Maybe she was struggling to get the cabinet making off the ground.

Maybe that was why she—

She opened her door, startling him out of his thoughts, and he realized he'd been silently parked in her driveway for far too long. Too long to open her door for her, too long because he knew it had made her feel insecure when she hurriedly said, "Well...um...thanks for dinner. I guess I'll see you around."

"Kacee—"

The door slammed shut, and she hurried up the driveway.

Quickly, he pushed the button to shut off the engine. Then he was out of the driver's seat, following her up the driveway, reaching her right as she started to unlock the front door.

"Sweetheart," he began. "I had a nice time—"

"Right." She pushed open the door. "Nice."

He caught her arm. "Yes, *nice*. But also fucking incredible. You're smart, Kacee. And funny and talented and can do a mean lawnmower." He stepped forward, drawing her against him. "Not to mention that you kiss like sin and have the sexiest pair of breasts I've ever seen."

Her lips parted.

Shut.

"*Ever*," he repeated.

"Charlie," she began, and her tone immediately set his teeth on edge. It was one of those things that his instincts knew immediately was trending toward martyr. An instinct that was confirmed when she said, "You know. It's probably better that we just call it here. You need someone—"

"Who stands up for me when she doesn't even know it's me?" he asked, stepping forward and pressing into her.

She backed up, colliding with the wood, her chin coming up, offering her mouth to him like he was a god and she was a virgin on the altar.

Pink and plump, damp and tempting.

"Someone who works hard and loves one of her jobs because it makes people smile, and the other because it makes people smile in a different way?"

Her lips parted. Her shuddering breath hit his skin.

"Or how about a woman who is talented and smart and I haven't been able to stop thinking about since the moment I collided into her?" He cupped her cheek, ran his thumb over her bottom lip so he didn't kiss her. Because he needed her to get this. To understand. To stop questioning and go with it. "I need you to listen," he ordered fiercely. "And listen good because I'm going to only say this one more time."

A flash in her eyes.

A fire that set him alight.

Good. He wanted that spirit, that ferocity. He wanted her to dish it out because he could take it.

"I like you," he said. "I like every bit of you that I've seen, sweetheart. Shy and quiet. Sexy and naked. Laughing and the tip of your nose rosy from the wine." He bent so that her eyes were aligned with his. "I like you, and I don't give a fuck that you didn't have a beer to offer me or that you think you smell bad after working your ass off. I don't care that you're worried ordering a steak or that your ex did something to fuck you up." Closer still. "I don't care about the past."

Her nostrils flared as she inhaled. "Charlie," she breathed.

Fucking nirvana hearing that soft, breathy way she said his name.

"I care about the woman in front of me," he said. "And she's fucking great. Do you hear me?"

"I—"

"Sweetheart," he gritted. "Do. You. Hear. Me?"

Her eyes narrowed. Her chin came up. "My ears work, don't they?"

His thumb ran along her bottom lip again. "I don't know, do they?"

Fire in hazel irises, pink flaring across high cheekbones. "I—"

He kissed her.

TWELVE

KACEE

Her fingers were tight in his hair.

His mouth was on hers.

His tongue darted in, tasting her deeply.

Her body molded to his, and she jumped, wrapping her legs around him.

Thank the sex gods, he didn't hesitate to hold her to him, one of his arms supporting her thighs, the other banding around her back.

Spice in her nose. Hard to her soft.

Then they were moving, and she distantly heard the door slam closed as he kissed her nearly senseless, as he walked down the hall with her playing pretzel. A moment later she was settled on top of something—on top of the granite counter of her island —and for once, she was glad that her house was empty.

There weren't any knickknacks or flowers or candles to move before Charlie pressed her back, laying her out on the counter like she was a charcuterie board and he was *all* about tasting those cheeses and meats and fruits.

He stepped close, hips between her thighs, his palms dropping on either side of her head, and he bent down, his breath puffing against her lips.

Her own lips parted, ready to taste—

And then *she* was tasting.

Or maybe *he* was tasting *her*. Because the kiss wasn't anything she was in control of. Not in the least. She was being devoured and owned, and not just by his mouth. His tongue stroked deeply, plundering her mouth, sending her head spinning.

Her fingers found their way back into his hair, clenching tight at the soft silk, her thighs squeezing around his hips.

Then *his* fingers joined the party, slipping under her hoodie, the tips grazing her abdomen.

She shivered, breath hitching when his palm flattened there, sliding over to grip her hip, tugging her up, arching her body so it was pressed even more tightly against his. It slipped beneath her, dipping into that space he'd created, dancing along the base of her spine, sliding under the waistband of her jeans.

Beneath her underwear.

Cupping her cheek, hot skin pressing into sensitive flesh, fingertips gripping her ass cheek, so damned close to the cleft between them that she shivered, especially when he began massaging deeply, drawing her cheeks apart, coming closer and closer to the damp heat of her pussy.

Damp?

Ha.

She was soaking. Absolutely drenched and dripping.

Her clit throbbed, desperate for that firm touch there. For fingers or tongue or his pelvis pressed to hers.

And he seemed to read that request, as though he'd picked it up from her brain when his tongue stroked against hers. Or maybe they were just in sync, in tune, sewn tightly together in a way that made it impossible for her to comprehend their bodies as two separate entities in this situation. They were one—intertwined and tangled together, working in tandem in a way that was instinctual.

Going with that mind reading or the utter *in sync*ness, his palm slid off her ass, around the front of her belly, drifting lower to the waistband of her jeans.

A flick and the button was open.

A tug and the zipper was down.

He reared back, dislodging her legs, but only for a moment. Because then he was gripping the top of her jeans, lifting her up, yanking the denim down her thighs.

She gasped when he popped one boot off, her jeans sliding off one foot.

Which was where he stopped disrobing her.

Or her jeans, anyway. Because next, he reached for the waistband of her underwear, and one jerk had them following her pants, sliding off her naked foot.

Leaving her pussy bare to his gaze.

And he *gazed*.

His eyes burned into her, palms coming to her thighs and spreading her wider, leaving her exposed and vulnerable under the bright LED lights of her kitchen.

"Charlie?" she began.

He didn't bring his gaze to hers, just kept staring at her pussy as he dipped a hand between her legs, stroking through the moisture and making her hiss out a breath as she arched, head falling back. "Fucking beautiful," he murmured, thumb pressing to her clit.

Not gently.

Hard.

And perfect.

Not a teasing glance of a finger. Not a gentle circle intended to coax.

It was pressure and it was intense and...it was fucking *everything*.

She moaned, bucking against that pressure, seeking more. Charlie dropped to his knees, thumb still applying pressure in heavy strokes, rough ovals. "Right"—she gasped when he hit a spot that had her seeing stars—"oh, my *God*. Right there!"

He didn't delay or question or freeze.

He kept moving. *Right there.*

But he did make it better, leaning in to brush his mouth over her folds, to dip his tongue into her. The flat of it dragged up, joining his thumb, working in tandem.

And she jerked.

Because it was there.

Right there.

Pleasure lapped at her ankles, the tide increasing rapidly. Flooding the shoreline, splashing against her calves, her thighs, her stomach and shoulders.

Charlie could sense that because he didn't stop the movement of his thumb, his words husky when he spoke against her, the hot puffs of air joining the flicking, the pressure, the rhythm that never faltered. "That's it, sweetheart. Come on my tongue."

She shivered.

Jerked again.

That wave of pleasure crashing toward her, engulfing her in a hard wave of sensation from head to toes.

It was abrupt and too intense and froze her lungs.

She couldn't breathe.

Not when her heart worked too hard, not when pleasure had every nerve in her body frozen in shock.

Panic gripped her for a moment.

But only a moment.

Because Charlie saw her through. She should have known that he would see her through, guiding her up and over and gently down the other side, pulling her up onto a blanket spread on the warm sand, the rays of the sun shining in the bright blue sky drying her, soaking into her skin and warding off the chill.

Fingers tracing random patterns gently on her thighs.

A mouth damp with her pleasure.

Eyes that were hot enough to leave her with a sunburn.

"Charlie," she murmured, reaching for his shoulders, tugging him up. He bent over her again, mouth slanting over hers for a kiss that set her blood on fire again. She gripped his shoulders, brought him down to her, his hard, warm body pressing into hers.

Her hands slid down his back, slipped forward around his waist and between their bodies, reaching for the button on *his* jeans when he froze—

"Charlie," she said again, concern now clouding the pleasure.

Had he—?

He reared back.

"What's that sound?" he asked, gaze bouncing around the room.

"What?"

He pushed off her, leaving her bare and exposed and... confused.

For a moment. *Only* a moment.

Because then she heard it. A sound that slid like ice through her, freezing her blood, crystallizing her cells, coiling sick sensation in her abdomen.

Then he was moving.

Sprinting toward the door leading out to the garage, whipping it open and—

"Fuck," he hissed.

She was thinking the same. Well, if she could think anything beyond the horror clouding her mind, *fuck* would be what she would be thinking and speaking and—

He moved again, dashing into the garage.

Where water was pouring into the space. Pouring. Like her own personal waterfall she didn't want any part of owning.

She stared at it for a long moment, that sick feeling growing.

Then she jumped to her feet, yanking up her underwear, fighting with her jeans and boot, tearing them off, not giving a shit that she was practically naked from the bottom down.

Because her cabinets were in there.

Her tools were in there.
Her *life* was in there.

THIRTEEN

CHARLIE

He hadn't seen that much water since...well since Niagara Falls.

Or at least that's what it seemed like when he darted through the downpour, feeling it instantly soak him to the bone, his clothes clinging to him, the rush of freezing water stealing his breath for one moment.

Then he got his shit together and began moving.

Slamming his hand on the button to open the door, hearing the whoosh of water having been dammed up now breaking free, and that whooshing sat heavy in his gut as he ran to the workbench on wheels, shoving it out of the garage, depositing it on the lawn.

Then he did the same to the next project—though it was made harder because this one wasn't on wheels.

Neither were the next three.

But he got them out, along with several expensive-looking saws.

A beat. Thinking. *Thinking*. Because he couldn't evacuate every single tool.

Tool...

Tool.

He'd had a leak like this a few months ago, a backup caused by tree roots, water pouring into his garage. It had ruined a couple of boxes of old crap from his childhood, nothing so important as what Kacee was building in her garage, but the point was that he'd had to call his landlord for help and they'd told him to grab—

Moving again.

To the workbench, searching for a wrench and hoping that a woodworker would have one...and stomach sinking when he didn't see one.

The door to the house whipped open the same moment he spotted an old, rusted toolbox in the corner of the space. He darted toward it, yanked open the lid, and found a wrench that would work the same moment that Kacee broke herself out of her trance and ran for the tool bench. They got tangled for a few seconds.

Her eyes were panicked. "I—"

He steadied her, hands on her shoulders, adjusting his grip so he didn't whack her in the head with the wrench. "Grab what you need," he ordered. "I'll turn off the water."

A beautiful mouth dropping open.

He shook her lightly. "Move, sweetheart."

Then *he* moved, running for the front of the house, shoving through the bushes and kneeling in front of large pipe coming up and out of the planter bed, a small shut-off valve visible before it curved and disappeared into the house.

The wrench onto the pipe.

Cranking it hard.

And...

The water slowed from a torrent to a rush to, by the time he made it out of the bushes, a trickle.

Thank God.

But he didn't stop moving.

There was still a shit-ton of water in the garage and a shit-ton of expensive tools and equipment currently exposed to it.

When he made it back into the water-damaged space, Kacee was still standing where he'd left her, horror tightening the normally soft features on her face. He wanted to comfort her, to go to her and take her into his arms, hold her close.

He didn't have time.

He needed to take care of her livelihood first.

So, he left her there and moved to the door leading into the house, propping it open. Then he brought everything he could carry into the house, lining the tools up on the counter. Rinse. Repeat. Until he'd cleared the bench. Until he'd cleared the garage as best he could.

Then he went out to the lawn for the saws, wrestling them into the house.

They lived in a safe neighborhood, but leaving the tools out on the lawn like offerings to whoever could haul them off wasn't a good idea.

He did the same with the cabinets, depositing them next to the saws in the living room, tucking towels under the wet bases, not knowing if he'd saved them or if it was pointless.

Then the lawn was cleared. The front door was locked. The garage was silent, the quiet only broken by slow and steady dripping.

And Kacee was standing silent and still.

Stunned.

He dropped a hand onto her shoulder, turned her slowly to face him. "Sweetheart," he began...and then he saw the tears. Streaming down her face, dripping off her jaw in time to those drops still falling from the sheetrock of the ceiling.

"Why?" she whispered. "Why does this always happen? Why do I work so hard an—and—"

Her face crumpled and he drew her against him, wrapping his arms tightly around her. He didn't know all that had happened to her, didn't know the answer to why whatever it was, was always happening to her.

He just knew that he had to hold her, had to keep her safe and comforted in this one moment. To take this bit of pain from her.

So, he held on tight.

And when she began crying in earnest, the sobs hitching her chest, her face pressing into his throat, he held on even tighter.

———

She was sleeping, curled up next to him, her arm slung over his middle, her head resting on his shoulder.

Half of his body was asleep—or at least, one arm and leg were.

But he wasn't moving.

Not with Kacee lying sprawled over him, breathing slow and deep, her eyelashes creating half-moons of black silk fanning along the tops of her cheeks.

She hadn't protested when he'd eventually scooped her up and closed the garage door the night before (leaving a tiny gap at the bottom, hoping that the ventilation would prove enough to stave off any mold until he could get a couple of fans in there).

She hadn't protested when he'd carried her up the stairs and into her bedroom when her sobs had slowed, setting her on the edge of the mattress and stripping off her clothes and replacing them with dry pajamas from her dresser.

She hadn't protested when he'd picked her up and crawled into bed, drawing her against him, and holding her tight.

She'd just...melted.

But not like she had the night before—not in response to his kisses or his mouth on her skin.

In exhaustion.

In...defeat.

So he'd wrapped his arms even more tightly around her and just held on, knowing there was nothing more he could give to her in that moment.

Just hold on, keep her close, draw a soothing hand down her spine over and over again until she finally let sleep suck her under. Until it was light out and they could deal with the mess downstairs. Until he found out what had brought this strong, beautiful woman to a breaking point.

Until he helped her patch up those breaks.

Handed her the mortar, the screws and boards, the supports.

Stood by, took her back.

Oh, he'd step in when necessary, that was for damned sure.

But he would also give her the space to do it herself. Because... he'd been there, been overwhelmed and stepped over, had his preferences ignored. It was important for him to stand on his own two feet, to do what he could. He was an adult, dammit. He could take care of his own shit. And she could, too. Not all the time, but at least he could let her try and then be there to support.

That was what he had always wanted.

Was that too much to ask for?

For Ji-Ho, it had been.

His way. *His* way. And Charlie wanting to do things his own hadn't jibed with that. Charlie wanting to do anything that wasn't Ji-Ho's own idea was an issue.

He'd let that go on too long.

But not anymore.

Not for himself.

Not for Kacee.

A hand shifting on his abdomen, dipping under his shirt, pressing against his skin, nails digging in slightly.

And then a gasp, Kacee sitting up, her eyes wide, her hair messy and in her face and—

She jumped out of bed, raced for the hall.

So quickly that he lay there, blinking in surprise after she'd been gone for several seconds before realizing that he was just sprawled in her bed, staring dumbly after her.

"Fuck," he muttered, shoving out of bed, feet hitting the

floor, wasting precious seconds for the pins and needles to fade so that he didn't fall flat on his face when he went after her.

Then he went after her, sole of one foot still prickling but with enough feeling that he made it down the stairs without killing himself. Into the hall...veering left because the kitchen light was on, the door leading out to the garage open.

He turned in that direction, hustled out, and found...

Her standing in the garage, enough moisture clinging to the air that he knew priority one had to be those fans, arms akimbo, face—when she slowly spun to face him—blank.

Then misery crept in, and her shoulders slumped. "Not a dream," she whispered. "Or not another nightmare anyway."

"Another?"

She strode toward him, face showing some emotion he couldn't discern, something that called at all the jagged parts of him, drew them forward, pricking all along the inside of his skin. Then she sank down onto the step, next to his feet, hands coming to her head, and a long, slow sigh wracking her frame. "Another," she repeated the word on a sigh that was short and quick but no less stark. Then her hands dropped and her gaze tipped up toward his in a way that had him sinking down onto the step next to her.

And waiting.

"I'm broke," she said. "Broke in a way that the hole I have to dig out of is deep and jagged with crumbling sides, making it hard as hell to crawl out of it." Her head shook. "Broke because I've worked my ass off for *years*, from the moment I was sixteen and emancipated myself out of the system. Broke because I put all of my money into buying this house and my ex stole my safety net—both out of my bank account and in the form of all the tools in my garage."

Fuck.

"So, I didn't have any money, didn't have any tools to work, and..."

"Disaster," he finished quietly.

A nod. "Luckily, I saw the listing for Goldie—well, to be a

mascot, anyway. Goldie, as I'm sure you know from Scarlett, didn't initially go as planned."

He smiled, inclined his head.

He knew that well.

There was a miscommunication between when the costume went live—mainly because Scar and PR Rebecca hadn't planned on having a giant gold turd be the new mascot for the team. They'd nixed it, ordered a new costume that was supposed to resemble an actual nugget.

But no one had told Kacee that.

She'd gone out there, owned the gold poop, and owned it so well that #GlitteryGoldieGuano had trended nationally, and fans had nearly rioted and demanded the original Goldie when the team had tried to debut the new and improved nugget costume.

Thus, Goldie, the glittering gold poop, stayed.

"Being Goldie meant that I could start buying the tools to replace what Robbie stole and sold on Craig's List. It meant I could keep working and digging myself out of the hole he left me in. I could pay the mortgage, my cell phone, and eventually the power, the garbage. Good internet is still out of reach, right along with any streaming service, new clothes, or food other than ramen. Every single bit that I've earned being Goldie has gone to keeping my head above water." Her eyes shot to the hole in the ceiling, where the sheetrock had given way the night before, gifting her a personal waterfall in her garage. "And just when I was getting ahead, when I was starting to dream—not big dreams," she added in a whisper, "just normal, everyday dreams. Food in my fridge. Watching bad reality TV. Being able to go to the movies." Her expression went unfocused, her voice softened. "I miss movie theater popcorn. It was always a treat because it's so damned expensive. But the butter, the *smell*. I loved that."

His heart squeezed tight.

He didn't come from a family that had been well-off. His parents loved money and spent it as though it flowed like water through their fingers. They'd had lean times and flush times, and he'd always been aware that the sense of security was a facsimile, a fragile one that could give way at any second.

"I want to get back to the point where I can go to a movie," she whispered. "Or just sit on my couch and watch TV with a glass of wine and not worry."

Such a simple request.

Small dreams. *Everyday* ones like she'd said.

Her voice dropped, becoming almost inaudible. "It's not for me." She sighed and pushed to her feet, disappearing into the kitchen.

By the time he made it up off the step, turning to follow her, she had returned, broom in one hand, mop in the other.

"Sweetheart," he began.

Glassy eyes met his. "Not now, Charlie. Please, just...not today."

So, he let it go.

Didn't talk about what she'd shared.

Didn't acknowledge any further than that *sweetheart.*

"Okay, baby," he murmured, taking the mop from her.

She gripped the broom until her knuckles were standing out in sharp relief against her skin, peaks of sharp white against soft olive. She watched him for a drawn-out moment, as though holding her breath, as though expecting him to break that gentle promise he'd just given.

When he didn't, when he just moved to the corner of the garage, starting to mop up the water that had pooled there (keeping her in view out of the corner of his eye so that he could watch the tension in her spine relax...marginally).

And with her face set in stark lines, she started cleaning.

FOURTEEN

KACEE

She'd expected him to leave.

Not to stay and mop.

Usually, the moment that the men in her life saw that exit, they took it and did it fast, tires squealing as they rounded the corner too fast.

Even after the floor was mopped and her tools were inspected, he stayed.

Well, he had gone for a bit while she'd taken apart her miter saw, reappearing with a trio of fans that he'd positioned around her garage.

Then, grabbing a towel and going over the tools on her counter, wiping them down until they gleamed, testing each one in the outlet, putting aside any that were broken (thankfully that had only been a pair of drills—and while painful because she couldn't afford to buy anything new, let alone a pair of drills that cost a hundred and fifty dollars...each, she was very aware that it could have been a lot worse).

A *lot* worse.

Her saws alone...well, suffice to say, the thought of having to replace them again had her breaking out into a cold sweat.

Luckily for her, while she'd stood like a giant, frozen dummy, Charlie had taken action.

He'd cleared the space, dragging out her pieces, her workbench with all her samples and drawings and her portfolios. Her saws and tools and—

He'd saved her.

In a world where she was used to saving herself, used to doing anything and everything on her own, crawling, clawing, *inching* toward everything she'd earned, he'd just given.

To her.

Her.

How? Okay, she knew *how*. He'd done all the things she should have done, and he'd done them without asking for thanks, without resentment, without hesitation.

Why?

That was harder to process.

It went back to the whole giving her the world thing. The assertion he'd made that had sent panic and worry and longing and fear all twining through her.

After the tools, he'd pressed a kiss to the side of her neck, said, "I'll be back."

And now he was back with several bags slung on his arms, marching through her front door like he lived there. His eyes hit hers and the warmth in them had her fingers slipping on the saw she was adjusting.

"Shit," she hissed, pain slicing through her finger.

"What?" he asked, bags hitting the ground.

"Nothing," she said quickly, pressing the injured digit to her side and finishing with the screw she'd been putting back in after drying it.

"What is it?" he asked, voice closer this time, the question a series of warm puffs of air on her nape.

"Nothing," she said again, "just pinched my finger—"

Before she could even finish with the lie, considering that she knew the slice from the saw blade wasn't "nothing," could feel the blood pooling up on the tip of it. Still, it wasn't anything that a Band-Aid wouldn't fix.

She'd had no shortage of pinches and cuts and the occasional stitch (or superglue because hospitals were expensive, especially for people with the bare minimum of a health plan).

This didn't require anything more serious than a bandage... and maybe a little superglue.

But Charlie didn't seem to know that.

He reached to her side, snagged her hand, and lifted it, eyes sparking, lips pressing down flat before he said, "*Nothing.*"

She tugged.

He didn't let go.

"Like I said, it's nothing," she repeated. "Let go, Charlie."

His fingers tightened. "Nothing," he repeated.

"Believe it or not," she said, her own temper sparking, "I *have* had a cut or two in my life."

"Right," he muttered, drawing her up onto her feet and into the kitchen, sticking her finger under the faucet, cold water pouring over the injury. "So where are the Band-Aids?" he asked after tugging out a bar of soap and washing her finger gently and more thoroughly than she would have bothered had she been doing it herself.

She thought of the ancient box of bandages currently residing under her sink in her bathroom, wondered if there were even any Band-Aids left inside it. "Umm..."

That *umm* was a mistake.

His eyes sliced to hers, reading the thoughts going through her mind with startling clarity, considering that he wasn't a mind-reader—or she didn't think he was anyway. "Let me guess," he muttered, reaching for the paper towel holder mounted to the bottom of her upper cabinets, tugging off the final half-sheet sitting on that roll (which, coincidentally, had been sitting on that roll for several months because if she didn't tug off that scrap then she didn't have to buy a new roll).

He glanced down at it, and she couldn't miss the frustration in his gaze, in his words when he proved that mind reading by saying, "Let me guess, the Band-Aids don't exist—"

"They exist," she began to protest. "They're below the sink in my bathroom."

"Okay," he muttered, "they do exist, but they're so old that when I open the box, a fucking bat will fly out."

She had been starting to feel annoyed—the man was proving to be bossy and pushy and—

Just *grr.*

But the bat quip had a giggle bubbling up in her throat.

She didn't let it loose, just swallowed it down and glared. "No bats."

A sniff before he gently wrapped her finger in the paper towel, taking her other hand, lifting it so that it was wrapped around the injured digit and exerting enough pressure to slow the bleeding but not so much as to hurt.

The man did that.

Seemingly without thinking.

Then he turned to the hall and she heard his feet on the stairs, leading upstairs, fading as he walked down the hall, no doubt into her bathroom and reaching into the cabinet beneath the sink.

A few minutes later he was coming down the stairs, that ancient box in hand.

It was dusty.

The blue strip on the top of the box almost gray from the amount of dust clinging to it.

Well, that didn't mean anything other than that it had been a long time since she'd had need of a Band-Aid. That was a good thing, right? It meant she didn't cut herself all the time.

Go her.

Then he tugged open the lid, dust poofing, and showed her the inside of the box.

One lonely bandage resided inside.

Maybe it was sad and lonely all by itself in the box, but she had one freaking Band-Aid so that was a victory, right?

It *was* a victory.

She smiled, showing off her pride in that victory.

Until he opened the packaging and the bandage pretty much disintegrated at the first touch.

Well...shit.

One red brow lifted, his mouth pressed flat, almost lost in the stubble of his beard. But she didn't need to see his mouth to sense his displeasure. It filled the air, tense and stiff and heavy. A spin and he turned, dumping the box and ruined Band-Aid in the trash and disappearing back into the hall. This time, though, he didn't head for the stairs.

He went straight toward the front door.

Out the front door.

It slammed shut behind him.

A bolt of despair. Leaving. Now. He'd had enough and he was leaving and—

So what? she thought, lifting her chin. If he left, she'd survive. Just because some sexy redheaded man with a gorgeous smile and sky-blue eyes liked her and promised her the world didn't mean that she'd go limper than a lousy crepe just because he walked out her front door.

She would survive.

She *always* survived.

Sexy, redheaded men with stubble that felt delicious when it brushed her neck as his lips hit her skin, who carried her when she had a meltdown all the way up her stairs and helped her into jammies and held her tight while she slept.

Would it hurt for him to keep walking out that door, hurt more than it should considering the length of time they'd been in each other's lives?

Fuck, yes.

But she was soaking in all that redheaded deliciousness.

She'd survive. She'd bank the good times to get through the bad.

The door opened, startling her. She heard it slam shut again, footsteps echoing down the hall *again*. But this time they came toward her, growing louder and more clipped as he made it into the kitchen. Eyes on hers, mouth flat, a red first aid kit in his hand.

A few seconds later it was open on the counter, shoved between a set of screwdrivers and her squares.

A few seconds after *that*, he was extracting several small butterfly bandages, one larger one, and a roll of gauze, along with a tiny pair of scissors and some adhesive tape.

She was blinking at the selection of supplies, the calm and steady way he'd laid them out, and so she almost missed the gentle way he peeled back the paper towel. But she didn't miss the careful way he applied the butterfly bandages, how he gently placed on the larger one. How he was still so careful and gentle when he wrapped her finger in gauze and secured that gauze with tape.

As his mouth dropped to her bandaged finger, lips gently pressing against the small hurt that she hardly felt any longer, she realized that the world wasn't always vast.

It could be as small as a kiss to a hurt.

As a first aid kit spread out on the counter.

———

"Absolutely not," she said later. "Absolutely *freaking* not."

It was later, but not *that* much later, though, just around lunchtime. Despite Charlie's attempts to shepherd her into her family room, to coax her back to her tools, with her finger cleaned and wrapped up, she'd finally processed—or more accurately, *remembered*—the bags that he'd walked into her house with.

Bags that, consequently, were filled with food.

Food that wasn't from the dollar store, food that definitely wasn't instant ramen.

It was fruit and veggies, salad mix and dressing, cereal and rice and pasta and meat, condiments and paper towels and napkins and toilet paper, and in the second set of bags Charlie had just walked back in with—hanging from his wrists like oversized bracelets and identical to the bags sitting in the corner of her kitchen—laundry detergent and bleach and garbage bags...and two identical drills to the ones that hadn't worked.

That was when she had lost her collective shit.

Or maybe it was when he pulled out a box of movie theater popcorn from the food bags.

Or maybe...it was all of it.

Too much.

"You need to take this back," she sputtered as he dragged a bag toward him and began unloading more fruits and veggies into her fridge.

"They're groceries, sweetheart. They don't exactly have a return policy," he said, opening the freezer and throwing in some bags of frozen vegetables and microwave meals and smoothie kits —and thank God some of the food was going in the freezer. She could have salads for days and still not make a dent in what he'd brought.

No.

Not *thank God*.

The man had some balls on him, just waltzing in with the entirety of Whole Foods on his arms.

"Well, the drills do," she said. "I'm damn sure Lowe's has a return policy."

"They do," he allowed, slamming the fridge closed and moving with a new bag to her pantry. "But considering I bought the drills months ago thinking I'd help Scar with her house, but never got the chance to actually open them since the team and their intervening has exceptional organization skills and they put me to work in ways that didn't involve drilling holes, that return window closed a long time ago."

That was a lot to process, and by the time she did, all she could say was, "Oh."

"Yeah"—he slammed the cupboard, bunched up the bags—"*oh.*"

She glanced around the space, saw that everything was put away, and sighed.

"Does that sigh mean that you're going to let this go?"

Irritation bubbled into rage that she knew was unreasonable considering the man had been nothing but nice to her. Nice and considerate and...*nice.*

Also, this just in, apparently rage significantly limited her vocabulary.

"Let it go?" she asked, pushing off the counter and walking toward him. "Let. It. *Go?*"

His fingers hit her cheek, drifting across the skin there, tucking a few loose strands of her hair behind her ear. "Yeah, babe. It's in the fridge, the freezer, the cupboards. I'm not taking it back. You need food that's not ramen, and I'm in the position to give it to you—"

"But—"

"One day, you'll be able to give that to someone else," he said, hand shifting so that he was cupping her cheek, "and because you're you, I know you'll give that back."

Her lungs froze.

"So accept this," he murmured, the words sinking into her slowly, intently, as though she were slowly lowering herself into a bathtub filled to the brim with hot water. A burn then a slow heating, soaking through her toes, her legs, her stomach...her heart. "Just accept it, sweetheart," he said softly and she shivered at the warm, intent tone, the voice that she thought might be able to smooth over all her rough edges, to talk her into anything. "And just pay it forward when you can."

Anything.

That had common sense reigning supreme, had her stepping back.

His fingers tightened slightly, as though he weren't going to let her go, and panic warred with the need to lean in, to let him hold her.

Then common sense reared up again and she slid away from him.

"Fine," she snapped. "I'll accept the groceries." A beat. "And the drills."

"And so graciously, too."

She narrowed her eyes, didn't acknowledge that snark. "But no more. Nothing else, Charlie. I mean it."

He shrugged, continued shoving the bags into each other until he had one big bag of bags, but what he didn't do was commit to the *nothing else* she'd demanded.

"Charlie," she began.

The doorbell rang.

And she saw red.

FIFTEEN

CHARLIE

His girl had a temper.

He had to admit that he liked it—something he probably shouldn't admit to enjoying, especially after the abuse Ji-Ho had hurled at him and attributed toward his bad temper (and never him).

But Kacee's temper was different.

She stomped around after realizing the doorbell ringing had signaled lunch being delivered, gathering plates from the cabinets and setting them down (firmly) on the counter, grumbling to him about spending too much money on her, glaring when he told her again to deal with it, and then serving him up two slices of pizza to her one.

Glaring even more fiercely when he tossed another piece on her plate.

Jaw working ferociously when she clenched her teeth into the slice and tore off a chunk...and then moaned in pleasure.

Her temper gone.

Mostly.

Because her "thank you" was pert.

But then because her fridge and pantry were full, she'd surprised the shit out of him by whipping up the best chocolate chip cookies he had ever tasted.

Then she'd shoved a dozen at him and told him to get lost while she got back to work on her saws.

He left her then...but only to head into the garage to move the fans around and check on the walls. They were drying well, and he didn't think they would mold. The moisture in the air had dissipated, and with the exterior door cracked and the fans going, it seemed about as good as it would get.

At which point, he'd gone back into the house, ignored Kacee glaring at him as he finished organizing the tools on her kitchen counter before joining her in her living room, and peppering her with questions.

Which she answered prickly.

Until she relaxed, that was, her fingers still working on her tools, adjusting belts, taking pieces off, cleaning them, and then putting them back on. This coalesced with him asking her about her current projects, encouraged her to tell him about all the little details when she began to shy away from talking too much.

She didn't get it.

Didn't get how much he treasured the excitement that crept into her voice when she chattered about her projects.

The brightness of her eyes. The way that bright chased the shadows away. How her shoulders relaxed when she was talking about wood and clients and the right type of nails to use. That bright filled *him* up, made him want to give her that, give *him* that, to chase that high forever.

But, for the moment, he'd take listening to her talking about nails.

Tomorrow, he'd tackle the rest of it.

Because he had a long list of ideas to keep bringing that brightness...and he looked forward to her bringing that sweet, spicy, glare-filled temper in response.

"What about this one?" he asked when she'd finished with the saws and moved to the cabinets. The damp parts now dried out and in the process of being replaced or repaired. "How did you get it so soft?

No joke, the wood felt like velvet.

Her lips twitched, and she nodded at the block of wood—covered in sandpaper that she'd set him working with—in his hand.

"Lots of using that hand."

He smirked.

She sighed and shook her head. "Men."

Not able to resist, he leaned in and slanted his mouth over hers. She tasted like chocolate and the beer he'd picked up, not a combination he'd ever thought would have worked, but one that did. One that worked really freaking well. One that tasted like nirvana. One that—

Had him forgetting his thoughts and just focusing on her.

On the feel. The touch.

The taste.

On Kacee.

"I think you like *this* man," he teased, words soft and their lips brushing as he spoke.

Her shoulders went stiff.

She pulled back, gaze going to her hands, to her wood, to the drawing with measurements labeled that she'd gotten out earlier to show him how the finished armoire would eventually all come together.

Basically, anywhere but where he wanted it...which was on him.

Two choices—he had them. Push more, or back off.

He'd done a lot of the first, should probably take the tact of the second.

But he didn't have it in him. Which was why he leaned forward and cupped her jaw, tilting her head—gently but firmly since she fought him—until she was meeting his gaze. He started to ask what was the matter.

He knew, though.

She'd cracked open the door.

He was getting in.

She liked him, and...that terrified her.

So, he just laid it out. "Have I given you any indication that I'm not in the same boat, sweetheart?" he asked, thumb rubbing lightly over her skin, knowing she felt his touch and did it deep when goose bumps prickled to life on her skin. "I like you. I've told you that. I've made it clear. I get this is new and intense and I don't know where we'll be in six weeks, let alone six months or years."

Well, the last was a lie.

He knew where they would be, knew where he wanted them to be, and that was together with her in his bed every night for the rest of his life.

But he'd been there before.

He'd had that longing and those dreams, and they'd imploded.

He knew that Kacee was different, knew she was special and more and that he wanted her, wanted that forever, but he was also intimately aware of the fact that forever didn't always last... forever.

So, he didn't make empty promises.

He gave her the now, the promise of the future.

"But I know where I want to be, if it continues to go good between us," he said, leaning closer and rubbing his jaw against hers. "And that's right here, with you close, watching your face light up when you talk about work and soaking in your smiles."

Her lips parted, breath shuddering out and glazing his skin. "Oh," she whispered.

He pressed his lips to the hinge of her jaw. "Yeah," he said again. "*Oh.*"

Another shiver and then she was straightening, leaning back and narrowing her eyes. "You're far too charming for your own good."

Laughter in his throat, chuckles rumbling up and dancing off the tip of his tongue. "That's the best compliment you could give me, sweetheart."

A glare.

One that was undercut by a smile that sent his pulse skyrocketing. An order followed that had desire flooding his veins, dancing along those buoyant donut-shaped cells like it was a series of rafts navigating class four rapids. "Well, if you really want to see where we're going, where we're going to be in six weeks or months or years"—his heart squeezed because, fuck, he liked the sound of that—"shouldn't you come here and kiss me?"

Who was he to ignore such an order?

He leaned close.

Their lips met.

Their kiss started soft and light...and ended with chests heaving, Kacee with her shirt off, and his cock hard and aching.

And this was because he'd miscalculated.

The doorbell rang. Once. Twice. Both of which he ignored.

At least until his cell began blowing up and he remembered that he'd called in a favor...and that favor was in the form of Kaydon and Scar.

The doorbell went again.

"Fuck," he muttered, finally tearing himself away from the temptation that was Kacee.

"What?" she murmured dazedly, reaching for him again, her fingers grazing the top of his pants.

"*Fuck,*" he muttered again when her fingers slipped beneath the waistband of his jeans and brushed the head of his cock. Not hard since it was...well, *hard* and doing its level best to escape his underwear and jeans and find its way into the glorious hot, wet heat of her pussy.

The doorbell went one more time. His phone rang again.

His sister wouldn't give up. Not when he'd gone out to dinner with Kacee the night before. Not with the scene in the new changing room, him basically staking his claim. Not when she knew the barest details of Ji-Ho and the disaster that had been and she had Kaydon and her happy ending, which meant that, of course, she wanted everyone around her (and especially her brother) to be happy too.

Hating his life (and not exactly hating his sister, though he was definitely filled with intense annoyance), he fixed the bra he'd been in the process of divesting Kacee of, grabbed her shirt, and tugged it over her head.

Was it inside out?

Yes.

But his sister and her man—and subsequently, the whole of the Gold team—had more things to talk about aside from Kacee's inside out shirt.

Or so he hoped.

"What's the matter?" Kacee asked, stumbling to her feet, the haze of desire fading.

"How's the temper?" he countered, wrapping her hand in his, tugging her to the front door.

Brows drawn together, wide hazel eyes on his, swollen and objectively still kissable, lips parting to ask, "What do you mean?"

"You'll see," he muttered.

He tugged open the door.

And felt his own eyes go wide.

Because it wasn't just Scar and Kaydon on the porch.

It was...*everybody.*

Or it seemed that way, anyway.

Fanny and Brandon. Scar and Kaydon. Josh—a newer defenseman on the team that Charlie just barely knew. Brit, Stefan, and their newly adopted baby. PR-Rebecca and Kevin and *their* baby. Logan and Char. Liam and Mia. Blue and Anna and Blane and Mandy and their respective kiddos. Calle and Cooper and their plus one. Mike and Sara...

And more, but he lost count, mainly because they barreled into the house, arms full of babies or toddlers or bags. Coop and Liam held a TV. Blane a toolbox as he brushed past Charlie and

Kacee and pushed through the gathering in the hall, disappearing to locations unknown inside the house. Stefan and Max (with Angie supervising) didn't join the throng. Instead, they moved to a stack of sheetrock in the driveway.

Distantly, he heard the garage door opening, watched Blane walk out to join them.

"You did this?" Kacee whispered, when the mass of humanity had disappeared.

"I...um...I called my sister, asked her to bring her spare TV over," he said. "That's it. The rest of it—"

What the fuck was the rest of it?

The Gold, he supposed.

The team that was family, that banded together and got shit done.

And when they heard that one of their own needed something—whether it was one of the housekeeping staff whose son needed hockey equipment or their publicist who needed assistance with her house or their mascot who just needed a little help because she'd been put through the wringer by her ex. It was chipping in with babysitting. It was setting up meal trains when someone was sick or having a baby or was just overwhelmed.

It was team barbecues and secret Santas and Easter egg hunts.

A family that was made—and made into something special.

And he'd unknowingly unleashed them on Kacee.

Whose face was pale.

But only for a moment. Because then murder crept into her expression.

Sixteen

Kacee

She was going to kill him.

A slow dismember. An even slower decapitation trailing several painful and bloody dissections. Then maybe she'd light him on fire.

Yeah, Charlie ending up as ash would work for her.

And yeah, her violent, bloody thoughts were the source of some concern in her mind.

But she was going with it.

God knew she had the tools to get that shit done.

A screech—happy, angry, she didn't know. She only knew it belonged to a child and her family room was filled with saws and her kitchen with tools and—shit—kids, especially the age of those that had just barreled beyond her, could do a lot of damage to themselves and others and her house with tools and saws and chisels and screwdrivers and—

Shit, she didn't have time to think about dismemberment.

She had to get the children out of the war zone.

Brit popped her head into the hall. "Hi, Kacee. Excuse the Gold destructive wave." A smile that showed off beautiful white teeth (a misnomer for a hockey player, Kacee knew, though she suspected it had much to do with the fact that Brit wore a face mask *and* mouthguard). "The children have reconvened in the back yard until it's safe in here. Is that okay with you?"

Was it okay?

Nothing about this made any sense. Nothing about this was okay.

But what could she say?

These people were way higher on the pay scale than she was, so this had to be okay. Otherwise, they might not want her to be Goldie anymore, and she needed the money from Goldie and she really liked *being* Goldie and—

Brit's smile faded.

And she realized she'd just been staring and not answering.

Kacee shook herself, cleared her throat. "Of course," she said. "I don't really have a lot of kids' toys"—she didn't really have *any* kids toys—"but there's an old soccer ball out there, I think. And maybe a few Hula-Hoops."

Leftover from the previous owner.

Probably ready to disintegrate, and the ball was probably flat.

Brit spun to reveal a backpack hanging on her shoulders. "I've got it covered, and maybe if I get the kids busy, Mandy will give me back my baby."

Mandy popped her head out of the kitchen, holding a baby bundled in a soft gray blanket. "Not likely," she said, running her fingers down the baby's cheeks. "I miss this stage."

Brit frowned. "Get Blane to give you another one," she grumbled. "This one is mine."

"But Blane says we're done after I was so sick the last pregnancy." Despite her words—tinged with a bit of whine, they made a swap—baby for backpack. "But maybe I can convince him that adoption is the way to go." Mandy smoothed a hand over the peach fuzz covering the baby's head. "After all, it worked for you and Stefan. One day just the two of you, the next—bam!—the payoff of a baby with no morning sickness!"

She swept her arms out like she was a game show announcer.

With a grin and a flourish and a—

"Mom! I need my bubbles! Miss Mia said she'll show me how to round kick them if I can get the bottle."

Mandy's face went soft and she slid the backpack from her shoulder, digging inside until she unearthed a pink container of bubbles, handing it to her daughter with a soft, "Make sure you open those outside. Remember last time?"

A nod, a silky blond ponytail shaking. "It made a big mess."

Mandy nodded back, smoothing her hand down that tail. "And remember that we're here to clean up the big mess in Miss Kacee's house, not to add to it."

The little girl spun to Kacee, closing the distance between them, the bubbles clutched in her little hand, her expression very serious. "Did you not clean up your mess, Miss Kacee? My mom says that we always have to clean up our messes."

Her heart squeezed as she crouched down. "Well, peanut, my house decided to make the mess for me, so now"—she swept an arm toward the family room and then to the kitchen—"I'm working on it."

A sage nod. "I don't like it when my room gets messy on its own."

Mandy laughed softly.

"Not fair, is it, peanut?"

She shook her head. "Nope." She held up the bubbles. "I'm going to go play with these."

"Sounds good," Kacee told her. "And if you hit the switch by the double doors, you'll have more light to practice your round kicks."

"Okay!" She started to run down the hall, stopped and turned back. "My name is Madeline. Not peanut."

Kacee bit back a smile. "Well, hi Madeline. I'm Kacee."

"I know."

Then Madeline spun and hustled down the hall, out of the kitchen. Kacee watched her pause and study the light switch by the double doors, smiled when she jumped up and hit the lever, illuminating the back yard. A good thing since it was nearing winter and the sun was setting earlier and earlier.

"Bubbles!" she heard the kids yell.

Mandy winced. "I should probably go supervise considering that two of those belong to me."

"Stay a little longer," Kacee found herself offering. "It sounds like there are plenty of adults out there."

Brit nodded. "Plus, Mia wrangles little ones for a living." She glanced at Kacee. "Mia is a karate instructor and owns a studio in the city." A nod to the cupboards. "Which one has the wine glasses?"

Heat on Kacee's cheeks.

She had wine, thanks to Charlie.

She also had only *one* wine glass, thanks to her past adventures bingeing *Holiday Baking Champions* with that glass in one hand and shoveling popcorn in with the other.

"I, um, only have one." She cleared her throat. "Single woman and all that—"

Mandy lifted a brow. "Single, are you?"

Her tone said she didn't think single was on the table, and it probably wasn't considering Charlie had activated the Gold crew and her house was now filled with sexy hockey players (Brit included because all that lean strength was pure yum) and their gorgeous wives, girlfriends, partners, and fiancées.

But she and Charlie were...

Something.

And she wasn't sure that *something* was quantifiable into boyfriend and girlfriend.

Brit's eyes widened, both of her brows lifting in question.

Kacee's cheeks got somehow even hotter. God, they had to be fire engine red by now. "Well, I mean...I—" She coughed. "Charlie is—"

"She hasn't decided if she wants me to be her boyfriend yet."

She jumped at the sound of his voice very near her ear, melted when his hand hit her waist, drawing her lightly back against him. Like there was an invisible string connecting them, drawing her in, melding them into one being, making her feel like finally there was one person on this whole planet who might look into her soul and see her as...her.

And not run for the hills when he did.

Who might surprise her and stay.

Hope wove through her middle, stitched itself into her heart, and did it deeply.

She swallowed, really liking that sensation, but also deciding to ignore it. Because if she focused on it, focused on the joy that gave her, then she might be the one running for the hills.

Then she found herself, found her sass, found her inner Goldie.

Her chin came up. "Well, funny story, since he's so communicative that he invites the entire team over without mentioning it to me"—she slanted a look (okay a glare) at him that had Brit and Mandy choking back laughter—"but the man hasn't asked me for anything besides out to one dinner."

Brit's forehead went wrinkly, even as her lips twitched.

Mandy wasn't so circumspect. She burst out laughing. "You'd better watch out with that one, Charlie. I don't even think Scar can spin that sass."

A thread of guilt had her saying. "It was a very nice dinner, despite the twenty-five-dollar salads." She cleared her throat. "One that was followed by him saving my livelihood," she admitted. "So, I can't be too mad. He earned his keep."

Charlie chuckled softly, and she shivered when his lips brushed the skin behind her ear. "Good thing that pipe burst, considering my tongue in your pussy didn't register on that list at all."

Heat.

From head to toe, flooding her with need, making her thighs quiver, her ass tip back slightly.

And hold back a gasp when it encountered his long, hard cock.

Because she was remembering all the things she'd wanted to do to him the night before—her mouth on that cock, her tongue tracing every rigid muscle on his sexy body, *his* hands on her hips, pounding into her, his mouth on her skin, his cock stretching her, pounding home—

"And now I really want to know what he said," Brit stage-whispered—which was to say it wasn't a whisper at all.

Great.

Now Kacee was blushing again.

"I think we know what he said," Mandy quipped. "Or the gist of it, anyway."

"How?" Kacee blurted.

"Your shirt's on inside out." Mandy winked. "And it took you an hour to answer the door. It's not rocket science, babe."

Kacee tried to step away from the closeness of Charlie's hold—because God kill her now. Oh, maybe not, maybe she needed to survive long enough to run into her bedroom and fix her T-shirt, to turn it the right way. But Charlie's arm tightened, held her firmly against him. "I wouldn't do that, sweetheart," he murmured. "Not unless you want to give them *a lot* more to talk about."

It took a moment for that to process.

And a slight press of his hips—of his hard cock against her ass.

Then even more heat—embarrassment and need all tangled up together.

Charlie chuckled, giving her a whole different kind of heat, this time of the damp variety puffing into her ear and sending shivers down her spine.

Then he chuckled again, probably feeling those delighted shivers, grr.

But she wasn't a wilting flower. She was a hardy cabinet...or whatever the equivalent of a tough, kickass survivor who didn't fall apart just because a little extra pressure was put on her edges, her top. Which was why she spun in the circle of his arms and jabbed a finger into his chest, snapping out, "You're on your own with that."

A nip to the top of her ear. "God, I hope not."

"Ow!" she hissed, rubbing the small hurt.

"Yeah," he muttered, "tell me about it."

That nearly made her laugh, but she bit it back, glaring at him instead, opening her mouth to tell him to keep his teeth to himself—

He kissed her.

No warning.

Just bent and slanted his lips to hers and slid his tongue into her mouth...and she forgot about Brit and Mandy and all the things they might talk about while aboard the Gold's gossip train. She forgot her house and garage and back yard full of kids and grown-ups and—

His body to hers.

His lips on hers.

His tongue gliding against hers.

His fingers sneaking to the edge of her T-shirt—

Her *inside out T-shirt*. Her house full of people. Her *kitchen* full of people.

"Wine!" she gasped, tearing her mouth away from Charlie's, tugging out of his hold, leaving him and his hard cock to fend for itself. Which he did by turning for the counter and opening another bag—and seriously, when did he sneak that in? He dug around inside it, pulling out some red plastic cups.

Kacee winced as she glanced at her visitors—a group that had grown in her time kissing Charlie. Expanding to include Stefan, who'd swooped up the baby and was rocking him gently, and Blane, his jeans covered with sheetrock dust, and Coop, tall, with lean strength, a jaw that was so cut it practically begged for a woman's lips. She glanced from the group to her cupboard—the cupboard with only one wineglass. These people had money, professional athlete money, and they were probably used to drinking out of crystal. Not out of plastic. Not sharing one wine-glass. Not—

"Incoming," Charlie called, tossing the container of cups across the room.

Like the badass hockey goddess she was, Brit caught the package.

One-handed with a bit of flare, just like on the ice.

A second later, she had the plastic tie open and was tugging out cups for her and Mandy and the guys. Then Charlie went to a drawer—unerringly telling her exactly how much snooping and remembering the man had done in the time that he'd been unpacking all those bags—and pulled out a wine opener.

He went to work on the bottle, removing the cork, walking over, and filling their glasses.

"Thank God it's Cheat Day," Brit said, scooping one up. She inhaled deeply and then drank just as deeply.

"Sorry about the plastic cups," Kacee murmured as Mandy drank from hers.

Brit shrugged, nonplussed. "Trust me when I say I don't care about the vessel," she said, taking another sip. "I'm just happy to have something transferring the liquid into my mouth."

Coop started chuckling.

Calle strolled into the room, carrying her daughter on her hip. "What's funny?"

Brit jabbed a finger in his direction. "Don't you *dare*, Cooper Armstrong!"

Coop's mouth twitched as he snagged his daughter and gave his wife a cup of wine, all in one smooth, instinctual, *trained* movement.

"Daddy!" the little girl said, throwing her arms around his broad shoulders.

"Emma!" he said back, smoothing his hand over her hair.

"Maddy has *bubbles!*"

"Bubbles?" he asked.

"Yes!" She threw both hands in the air, totally trusting that her dad would keep her safe, and that trust revealed so blatantly, so easily had Kacee's eyes pricking.

She was thrilled—*thrilled*—Emma had that.

She was also sad—torn up—that she never had.

Which made her feel like a mean, jerky cow, but half of being a jealous jerk was admitting it, processing the feelings, and then moving on.

Fingers on her nape, gently pushing her ponytail aside, cupping the skin there.

Charlie.

She glanced up at him, fell into those blue eyes, and thought once again that, perhaps, he could read every thought sliding through her mind.

His fingers tightened.

A pulse of warm slid down her spine.

"*Lots* of bubbles?" Coop asked, drawing Kacee's gaze back to father and daughter.

"*So* many bubbles," Calle quipped.

"Bubbles!" Emma yelled.

Coop grinned. "Should we go see those bubbles, baby girl?"

Emma shrieked in answer...and in plenty of excitement.

Charlie's fingers tightened, his body shifted closer, his jaw brushing lightly against hers.

And for a moment, Kacee was in that cocoon, surrounded by that warmth. Protected. Trust coating her like a second skin.

"We'll leave Brit to all that *liquid* going down her throat."

Stefan choked.

Mandy giggled.

Charlie chuckled.

Coop caught her eye and winked. "And Kacee to turn that shirt right-side out."

Heat on her cheeks, and maybe she should have been more embarrassed because clearly everyone knew exactly what she and Charlie had been doing before they'd taken an eternity to answer the front door. But somehow in the last few minutes, being surrounded by the teasing and the banter and the adorable little Emma had relaxed her, and then Coop *including* her in that joke made her feel like for that moment she was part of something.

Something good.

Something warm.

Something that might be like family.

Something that gave her hope.

SEVENTEEN

CHARLIE

He watched Kacee work beside Mike, Blane, and Stefan (Brit having commandeered their baby and joined the back yard bubble—for the kids—wine—for the grownups—party).

Quiet to start.

Shy and uncomfortable.

And then a glimpse of Goldie.

Charming a laugh out of Mike, chuckles out of Stefan. Her shoulders relaxed. The tension left her spine, and more Goldie emerged.

After Coop had left the kitchen with Emma in tow, Blane had asked Kacee to come out to the garage. There was discussion over the sheetrock and whether it was worth salvaging the pieces that had gotten wet, cutting the others that were looking worse for wear after the day of moisture (despite the fans).

In the end, it was decided to replace it all. Kacee protested, which Mike, Blane, and Stefan had ignored, not because they didn't want her input, but because a giant pile of sheetrock and a dumpster had been delivered in front of the house and they didn't want it to "go to waste."

Which meant with a dark look over her shoulder at him, Kacee had relented, mostly because of the waste part, he knew, but then she had gone inside and come out with the drills—sending him a dirty look that told him it was also because of the free stuff and labor part—as she unboxed them and set them to charge. Another disappearing act before she had come up with some box cutters, a few pry bars, and she and the guys had gotten to work tearing off the sheetrock.

He'd been relegated to tool organization in the house.

Justly so, he supposed, considering his first—and only—use of the box cutter to slice through the sheetrock had nearly ended with him nicking a cluster of electrical wires.

He could man a drill—if he ever bothered to take them out of the box.

He could fix the washer on the sink to stop the faucet from leaking.

He could change a light bulb, swap out a switch plate, hang a perfectly straight picture.

But box cutters into sheetrock, and doing it while avoiding electrical wires...nope, not so much. So, tool organization. He'd get those suckers to shine—even if they didn't need to shine to be functional—and he was doing just that when his sister walked into the room, picked up another towel, and started buffing chisels.

Charlie turned his head, lifted a brow. "You had to call in the full Gold cavalry?" he muttered dryly.

A shrug. "She's got to get used to it sooner or later."

"I asked for a TV."

Another shrug. "And you got the full Gold cavalry." A grin. "Deal with it."

"Oh, I'm gonna deal with it," he said, well, *muttered*, because he'd started with the grumbling and wasn't going to stop. Not with his sister and her well-meaning interference (and did he know a few things about well-meaning interference? Yeah, so what? That wasn't the point). "I'm finally getting her to trust me," he said. "I had to fight with her to get her to accept my help at all, let alone the couple of bags of groceries, and here you are with the whole team, showing up like you're on the set of a house remodeling show."

"Funny how that works," she said with pointedly lifted brows.

He hated—no, he didn't *hate* anything about his sister—strongly disliked, yes. But only because she was right—and had been on the receiving end of a house remodel, courtesy of the Gold cavalry, not long before.

He knew she'd fought it for about ten seconds then had given in. Because she would have lost anyway—and because it was one of the nicest things anyone had ever done for her.

That had been his first foray into the world of the Gold and their awesome busybodyness. He'd loved that Scar had a real family, loved that she had a man who gave so much of a damn about her.

Scar deserved every bit of light shining in her direction.

He just didn't realize he had been folded into the...well...fold.

And that made him feel—

A lot.

Even more so to know that Kacee had been, too.

"Do you concede that point, bro?"

He frowned.

She grinned in that triumphant way that only sisters who'd scored a point could. "I *so* did," she said on a laugh. Then her face grew serious. "Also, why did you need to fight with her about groceries?"

Now he was the one with pointedly lifted brows. Growing up, their parents had made decent money, but spent it like it would burst into flames and turn to ash if it wasn't immediately used to buy expensive clothes or jewelry or new cars every two years. That had meant things had been tight growing up, tight enough that sometimes there wasn't food in the cupboards. It also meant that he instinctively knew the shame Kacee had felt in not being able to provide the beer she'd offered. Things had been tight enough that when he and his siblings grew up enough to have jobs and worked for their own money, that money had become room and board...even though they weren't adults yet.

And when his parents found out about his sexuality, they hadn't been the least bit supportive. The parental "care" had ended. All because he wasn't quote-unquote *normal* (and seriously, thanks, assholes, like it wasn't hard enough being young and confused not quote-unquote *normal,* but to have his parents pile on their disapproval added a special brand of assholery to the mix).

"Charlie?" Scar set down the chisel, now buffed to perfection, and touched his hand. "Is it that bad?" she asked gently.

"She's proud," he said, shoving the thoughts away.

He'd dealt.

Scar had dealt.

And Heath had them, even from the other side of the grave.

Scar's face softened. "We know a little about that, don't we?"

He sighed. "Yeah," he whispered. "We know *all* about that." Then he smiled, determined to not think about the past, about that black hole that always sucked him down and spun him around, shook him violently like he was in a blender. "Doesn't explain the cavalry, though. I believe I asked for one spare TV, not a home remodeling crew and the Gold parade of kids."

"One," Scar said, ticking off on her fingers, "the kids are a good distraction for a woman who likes kids but is shy of the cavalry."

Charlie had to give her that one.

"Two," she said. "You mentioned sheetrock and moisture, and I know you had that leak in your place a bit ago, but my sisterly intuition begins pinging when hearing those two words, having had a fair amount of experience with those two things while remodeling my *own* house."

"We had fans and—"

"The fans were good," she said quickly, patting his arm in a *there-there* gesture that set his teeth on edge (and she knew it, based on the beatific grin she tossed in his direction). Then her face got serious. "Seriously, though, Char. You did good, getting all the stuff out, getting some ventilation going, taking care of Kacee. She's a nice person, always kind and friendly, but a little distant. I'm glad you were able to break through, especially if the reason she's distant is because she's struggling."

He thought of her ex, of the shadows in her eyes when she spoke of him. "I don't think that's the only reason she's distant."

A sad smile. "It never is."

She squeezed his shoulder and then went back to the chisels, and because he knew that she was feeling the same, missing Heath, missing the huge, endearing presence that was their brother, and the protection and unconditional love he'd doled out freely to them, Charlie moved beside her, bumped her shoulder with his.

Her smile didn't falter, but it did lose the sad.

And he knew his did the same when she murmured, "We got you, bro. She's in, and if there's one thing I know, it's that no form of wall"—she nodded toward the windows that looked out to the back yard—"will keep this cavalry out."

His gaze followed hers, and his smile grew.

Because Kacee's box cutter had been taken away from her and she stood in the back yard bubble party, arms overhead, her hips shaking, leading all the kids in a dance.

A Goldie dance.

She spun in a circle, smile on her face.

It was so bright, so carefree, so...amazing that he sucked in a breath and stood there, absolutely starstruck.

Scar rested her head on his shoulder.

"You did that," he whispered. "Thank you."

"No, Char-Char," she whispered back. "That is all because of you."

EIGHTEEN

KACEE

They'd had pizza twice in one day.

It was probably going straight to her ass, but she couldn't find the strength to care, not when she had a belly full of crunchy crusts and ooey-gooey cheese and spicy pepperoni and unctuous olives.

And she was starting to sound like a food critic—or at least pretending to be one in her head because she now had a TV again and good internet...and several streaming apps.

After the guys—Blue and his son, Aiden, Kevin, Logan, Max, Brandon, and Gabe, the team's doctor, joining the menfolk in the garage—tackled the sheetrock (and kicked her out before she could help with rehanging the wide and heavy sheets—she still wasn't sure exactly how they had managed that because she definitely wasn't down with people doing free labor for her, least of all using all that free labor to cover the walls of her entire garage), Mandy and Brit had come into the garage, handed her drill off to Coop, and taken her to the back yard.

There was a speaker playing music, bubbles being shot into the air at regular intervals, and Madeline had taken her hands, dragging her around and around in a circle while she'd shaken her little booty to the music.

And...she'd gone full Goldie.

Somewhere inside her, the giant, glittering gold poop resided and she'd busted out to the remixed, kids' radio version tune of *Wheels on the Bus*.

The wheels went 'round and 'round until Emma had joined in, snagging one of Kacee's hands from Madeline's grip, and they'd spun until she was dizzy and out of breath (also, damn, those girls had endurance).

Eventually, the song wound down, *Twinkle Twinkle Little Star* came on, and the girls had gone full bubbles, giving Kacee a break, during which she'd bent over, rested her hands on her knees, and sucked in air.

Being Goldie had not prepared her for the flurry of energy the kids of the Gold wrought. Though, she supposed they got it from their parents, considering the flurry of activity in her house.

The girls had only given her a few minutes before they'd gotten tired of bubbling by themselves and had dragged her back into the mix, Brit, Sara, Angie, Anna, and Mandy and several toddler booties joining the fray, and they'd all had a dance party until the sun had begun to set and the yard was getting darker.

At which point the kids had demanded *Frozen*, which she (with a little assistance from Brit, who'd been relieved of her baby by Scar, after the little nugget had been stolen by Sara, who'd been borrowed by Angie, snuggled by PR-Rebecca, sung to by Nutritionist Rebecca, kissed on the top of the head by Char, and cuddled by Anna...and probably held by a few of the other women in between) had hung up the TV that Kaydon had brought for her to borrow. Also, let it be noted *that* (the whole borrowing she was pretending was only borrowing since she had a feeling it wouldn't only be borrowing in the long run and that freaked her *way* out) was the only reason she'd allowed it to be lifted onto the mount her ex had so kindly left screwed into the wall.

Also, *borrowing* was why she'd allowed Brit to log into her streaming services—the kids needed their movies, after all—and why she'd gone into the kitchen and popped the popcorn Charlie had brought. The same popcorn she'd intended on packing up with the rest of his groceries and dropping off on his front porch because she didn't need a handout.

She did, of course. As much as she hated to admit it.

She'd been living on instant ramen for months. It was a miracle—and probably only thanks to Maddy and Jimmy and their frequent plates they'd sent home—that she hadn't ended up with scurvy or some random nutritional deficiency.

She'd been drowning and kicking as hard as she could with her legs, using *all* the arm strokes to just keep her head above the surface of the water, and frankly, as much as she liked to think that she would have managed to make it to shore, to keep treading water until she got there or made it to a buoy or a boat or—

Enough with the water analogy.

She hated that she had needed help.

But also—and perhaps even more so—she was touched that they had come for her. No notice. No expectations. Just giving and warmth and kindness and laughter and bubbles and dancing. So, she couldn't shit on that by being ungrateful or not wanting to push back or turning their kindness back on them.

No arguments—or, okay, just a few token ones because she had a feeling how much the sheetrock and dumpster cost, and the thought of it gave her hives.

She'd find a way to pay them back—and if not monetarily, then in Goldie duties or in cabinets or...babysitting, which wouldn't be the worst thing in the world, considering how awesome the kids were—toddlers on up.

Jasper, Blue and Anna's son, was a beautiful little boy with blond curls and crystal *blue* eyes. He'd also soaked up every second of the sheetrocking, the hanging of the TV experience, handing screws up, helping her search through her toolbox for the right-sized bolts to fit the TV onto the mount. He'd made a face at

Frozen but had loved when *Tangled* was played after that, giving her his best Flynn Ryder smolder and making the collective gathered in her family room (that had been cleared of saws and other dangerous equipment) burst into laughter.

Then pizza had arrived, along with enough breadsticks to feed an army, and all those still playing hockey were thrilled to indulge, minus Logan, who was good about sticking to the diet plan, saying he preferred to have the salad (um, what?) over pizza.

But he had the muscles to prove that the team's diet plan worked, and if his belly was happy without ooey-gooey cheese, then who was she to throw stones?

Now the water line had been repaired, her garage had fresh sheetrock, the dumpster had been loaded, the fans' cords coiled before they'd been put to the side, and all of her tools and projects had been brought into the garage.

Almost like nothing had happened.

Except that her tools were shinier...and better organized.

Turned out that Max—a purveyor of all things nerdy (and figurine-related)—was really good at organizing things. Her tool bench looked like a showroom. Everything clean and displayed for easy access.

Even the projects were carefully placed so they had the best light.

And she was ready to get back to work.

Minus the day lost to dance parties and pizza belly, she would soon be back on track, especially since the Gold brigade were packing up. Putting jackets on sleepy kids, scouring the family room for a missing shoe and sock, buckling babies into car seats. It was a flurry of chaos and noise and tears and snot and...family.

Then the door closed and the noise cut off and it was just her with Charlie.

Who'd given her one of the best nights of her life.

She'd danced and cuddled, eaten and laughed, drank wine out of a red plastic cup without feeling ashamed.

And felt like she belonged.

Even though she wasn't a six-foot, two-hundred-pound hockey player or a beautiful and charming wife or girlfriend, she'd felt like family.

For the first time ever.

So yeah, she couldn't say that this had been one of the best nights of her life. It *was* the best night. Ever.

Ever.

And she had the man who was flicking the lock on the door and turning to face her, caution on his face—probably because he expected her to give him shit or to throw up walls and bolt. She'd fought him over his help, over groceries, over the popcorn—the unpopped kernels of which still populated the bowls sitting on the family room coffee table. Which she now had, along with a sofa and new loveseat, her ancient Goodwill find joining the ruined sheetrock in the dumpster, since Blane had gone home and brought the one from his house, or rather from his garage because he and Mandy had just bought a new one and they hadn't had a chance to get rid of it yet.

Another give.

Another thing she needed to repay.

But...also a memory, and a good one. She wouldn't forget how the kids had sprawled around it, sharing those bags, kernels spilling onto the carpet, cups of soda getting knocked over.

And no angry adult voices.

Just gentle ones soothing the tears that had followed, paper towels unspun and used to mop up puddles, cups refilled.

Pizza consumed.

The Mighty Ducks (the original version because it was a chef's kiss of a movie) was put on TV.

Flowing conversation. More laughter and teasing and pointed questions about her and Charlie, gentle scolding when she shared what little there was to share (one date, he was nice and she liked him—Mandy especially seemed invested and wanted to romanticize their meeting...but how did one romanticize a collision and then long minutes spent with a can of deodorizing spray?).

Mandy was determined to.

Romantic notions aside—or she supposed, romantic notions at the forefront of her mind, Kacee found herself staring at the man who'd orchestrated this whole evening and felt...

A lot.

So much that she wasn't sure how to quantify it—or maybe she was a little scared to quantify it because they were big feelings, strong feelings, feelings that might leave her broken and shattered in the end.

If it didn't work out.

When it didn't—

No.

The word was sharp, almost whip-like as it traveled through her mind, snapping her out of that line of thinking.

She didn't want to think about that now, didn't want it intruding on her thoughts, ruining this night, ruining her memory.

"What?"

Soft fingers on her cheek.

She wanted a hundred more nights like tonight. A thousand. A million.

A lifetime of them.

Dreams. Fantasies.

Probably not a reality.

"You mad, sweetheart?"

Mad? She'd been embarrassed, scared, then charmed and wooed and touched. Any mad had faded far, far into the back of her mind, and it had been less about *mad* and more because she'd felt ashamed for the empty pantry, the bare fridge, the sparse furniture.

"Kace?"

She blinked, found herself in the warm summer sky again. Charlie's fingers brushed along her cheek, traced over her bottom lip.

That touch—light and gentle. His eyes—more gentle and

focused solely on her, making her feel like she was the most important woman in the universe. His body—warm and strong and so near hers.

His mouth—the same one that had made magic happen between her legs—curved up at the edges.

And she felt it.

Those big, scary feelings that wouldn't go away, that she wanted to think, and that crossed her mind anyway.

"Mad, baby?"

Mutely, she shook her head.

She was...in love with this man.

And she was desperate to keep it.

Nineteen

CHARLIE

One second, she'd had shadows in her eyes, tension fanning out from the corners, pressing her lips flat, and the next, she'd relaxed.

"Baby?" she murmured.

Heat cascading over his skin, arrowing down toward his dick.

God, he liked it when she called him baby.

Maybe even more than when she said his name.

Though definitely not when she moaned it.

And, look, he could be a caveman, be a possessive alpha *man* —even though Ji-Ho had said, had made him feel like he wasn't—

He cut that thought off at the pass.

Halted the cold trickling over his shoulder blades, threatening to pull him out of this moment. And he didn't want to be pulled out. He wanted to capture the look on Kacee's face, the softness, the warmth turning her hazel eyes more gold than green and brown. Like molten metal, the heat threatening to singe his skin.

He wanted to capture that look, to imprint it on his mind, to somehow make it into a photo he could have forever.

Well, the last, at least, he could do.

Charlie whipped out his cell, hit the camera, and snapped a picture.

Confusion on her pretty face.

He stroked the backs of his knuckles down her throat. "I had to."

"Had to what?"

Capture that look, remember it forever. But he had the feeling that him mentioning anything about *forever* would send her skittering for the front door, whipping it open, and dropkicking him out onto the porch.

"You're beautiful," he said by way of explanation, and then lifted his hand and traced the blush that appeared on her cheeks.

"You're pretty beautiful yourself," she teased, leaning slightly into his touch. Her lips curved. "For an assassin."

That lean slid right through him, trailed by that smile, both embedding themselves in his heart. "I *am* a beautiful assassin, aren't I?" he teased, his palm sliding along her jaw, dipping into her hair. "Though, I didn't get the chance to set up my swimming pool with sharks."

"I thought it was a lake." She stepped closer, until the front of her body was pressed to his.

He stroked his fingers through the silk of her hair. "Pool. Lake. Whatever."

"Too bad," she said, smiling. "I love sharks."

"You do?" he asked, incredulous.

A solemn nod, and then she shifted, dislodging his hand as she pulled out *her* phone, only it wasn't to snap a picture of him. Instead, she came in even closer, tucking her body beneath his and showing him the screen. "This here is Titanic, and she's a Great White Shark who's currently residing near Catalina Island, but she goes south to Guadalupe Island—which is where scientists think that Great Whites go to breed, though no one has ever actually seen a breeding event. And—*oh!* This is Penelope. She's a Tiger Shark and hangs out in the Caribbean, and I swear that one day I'm going to go there and scuba with sharks in the ocean and

—" She cut herself off and glanced up at him. "Sorry," she said, hurriedly shoving her phone away. "I geek out on three things— bad reality TV, sharks, and wood—and I can get carried away, most especially about wood and—"

He stifled a laugh, his mind going to an altogether different type of wood, one she was very talented at mastering—or at least at creating.

She nibbled at her bottom lip, seeming to notice that change in the direction of his thoughts—from aroused to amused, though he couldn't lie, all that talk of wood was arousing him again. Mostly because he couldn't *not* think about the way she handled the pieces, all that sanding and the wrist and forearm strength that might bring.

"And well, sharks and wood don't make sense," she blurted, shifting slightly, as though to pull away from him. He wrapped an arm around her, kept her close. "But I guess they kind of *do* make sense because people can nerd out about anything that want to, and, well, wood is amazing and transformative and my livelihood, but sharks are just as amazing as wood. And, oh my God, I need to stop saying *wood* before I think about—"

Her eyes sliced down.

He chuckled.

Her cheeks flared.

"Kacee?" he asked.

"Yeah?" she whispered.

"I'm going to kiss you now," he said softly, hand finding her hair again, his fingers pressing into her scalp, tilting her head back.

Hot hazel eyes on his. Lush lips damp and parted for his kiss.

He bent.

Slanted his mouth across hers.

The world went dark...or maybe it was just that *his* world got so bright that it focused solely on Kacee. On her silken tongue and soft lips. On the strength of her fingers where they gripped his shoulders, how they wove into his hair and tugged him closer when he would have released her lips, belatedly remembering that she needed things like, well…oxygen making its way into her lungs. His world had been reduced to a pinprick, but it was so bright that he didn't care.

Not when she moved even closer, her breasts flush against his chest, her pelvis aligned with his, brushing the hard, aching length of his cock.

He growled and brought her closer, coaxing her legs up so she would wrap them around his waist. Then he spun in the hall, intending to take them back into the family room, to plunk her on the couch and put on some documentary about sharks so he could make her smile, and then hopefully distract her while it played.

But her fingers gripped his hair again, tugged his face close to hers, words puffing against his lips. "My bedroom is the second door on the right at the top of the stairs."

"I know that, sweetheart," he murmured. "We don't need—"

"Bedroom. Second door on the right."

He opened his mouth to protest, but she spoke before he could.

"Need is different from want, Charlie," she said softly, her fingers releasing his hair, nails dragging lightly across his scalp before they smoothed along his jaw, tangling in his beard. "And I want, baby."

Lightning in his veins, desire coiled tightly like a snake ready to strike in his gut. "Kace," he said, covering her hand with his palm, holding her to him. "Just because I helped you doesn't mean you—"

"This isn't that."

He waited for her to say more, debated how much he should press. It wasn't like he didn't want her. Fuck, he was practically vibrating with the need to sink into the wet, tight clasp of her, to get his mouth on her skin, her breasts, between her thighs.

Her eyes hit his. Held.

"It's not that," she said again. "It's—" A shake of her head. "I want you," she whispered, "and I want to feel it again. To get lost in the moment, to not worry, to have you touching me and inside me and stroking deep. I want you to come in me and then hold me tight afterward. I want *you*, Charlie."

Those words.

They stuck deep, arrowing into his chest with all the force of a flurry of bullets.

That...God, for so long, all he wanted was *that*.

Someone to want him for him. Just Charlie. Not a Charlie that was a son who didn't fit with the image of what his parents wanted. Not a Charlie who wasn't the brother he should have been, who'd retreated and crawled into his own head and hadn't been there for Heath like he should have in the end. Not a Charlie who wasn't the partner he should be, who was a disappointment and didn't hold up his half of the relationship.

Weak.

Pathetic.

Not enough.

His hands tightened on her waist.

"Charlie?" she whispered. "You're hurting me."

He hissed out a breath, quickly dropped his hands and stepped back. When she teetered, he reached out and steadied her, making sure to do it gently. "I'm sorry," he whispered. "I didn't mean to. I-I wouldn't—" He clamped his teeth together, feeling the hot itch of shame beginning to gather between his shoulder blades. "I'm sorry," he said again.

He turned away then, dislodging her hands when she reached for him.

"Hey," she said. "It's okay. You didn't—"

His eyes whipped toward hers and she froze, one arm outstretched.

"It was just a little too much pressure. We were swept up in the moment..." Her words were quick, disarmed by a smile. Trying to make him feel better. Finding excuses for why he'd hurt her.

He'd. *Hurt*. Her.

That shame became more than a tickle. It was a burn, cascading along his torso, burning down his thighs, his calves and ankles, sparking out through his toes. It spread upward too, crawling up his throat, choking him, filling his mouth with hot embers and ash.

Coating his tongue, his teeth.

Making bile rise, his stomach churn.

"I need to go," he murmured.

"Charlie," she whispered. "I'm fine. Can you—can you tell me what's going on? Why you have that look in your eyes?"

He couldn't see his eyes, but he'd seen his reflection in the mirror enough times to know exactly what she was talking about, knew that she was seeing all the things that had haunted him for a lifetime, had been pushed to a breaking point when Heath died, and then shoved right over a cliff when things had gotten so fucked with Ji-Ho.

He didn't want her to see that.

He *couldn't* let her see it.

Not with shame swirling and burning and choking and—

"I need to go," he said again, only this time he said it as he walked toward the door.

"Charlie—"

He couldn't stop himself from glancing back. "I'm sorry," he whispered. "I-I can't do this."

"Can't do what?" she asked softly.

Dark nights, wanting to end it all, the sharp barbs always circling, always sinking their claws deep into his mind, digging deeply, painfully, until he'd been so consumed by the thoughts, by the disappointment and anger directed at him that he'd half-expected to find himself bleeding from the ears, for it to be coming up through his throat, out his nose, dripping down and coating him like it was a second skin.

"I can't do this." Even to his own ears—free of dripping blood, but pulse pounding in their depths as his heartrate sped, as the panic and memories choked him—his voice was panicked. "I can't do *this.*"

"Charlie," she murmured, her expression so gentle that just looking at it made his throat close up, made his breaths feel like razors slicing through his lungs. She took a step toward him, but he backed up, whipped the door open, stepped through, hustled down the porch, along the driveway.

Trying to shove the memories down.

To forget.

Desperate to forget.

Then thanking God that his car was there so he could get in, drive off, and not have to think.

To remember.

To feel.

TWENTY

KACEE

I f she didn't know what inner demons looked like, the scene
would have wounded her.

Deeply.

She'd offered herself up to him—almost twice now—and basically asked him to fuck her, and even though the first time had
been interrupted unknowingly by Scar (and maybe she should
just stop with the whole propositioning thing because apparently
her luck was not good when it came to asking men to fuck her),
this time was something completely different.

Panic.

Regret.

Guilt.

All blowing across beautiful blue eyes like thunderstorms
marring the bright summer sky.

Then he left, the door slamming closed behind him, leaving
her staring after him.

She went for her shoes, was pulling them on, intending to
march over to his house and make him explain himself or to find
absolution in her saying that she was fine and it wasn't a big deal

(all while knowing that she had no right to say the latter, nor to tell him how to feel). When she heard his engine turn over, she remembered that he'd driven back to her place.

With the groceries.

With the drills.

With a band of helpful Gold gossip mongers on his heels.

And a TV and pizza—twice—and movies and adorable little kids and bubble parties and a garage that was completely set up for her to go back to work and—

Her delaying in putting on her shoes cost her...cost *him*.

She made it to the door just as he reversed out of her driveway and took off down the court, taillights disappearing into the night, knowing that her plan of walking to his house and knocking on the door until he answered (thus allowing her to get to the bottom of things) had gone to shit.

"Shit," she muttered, turning back into the house, seeing the family room cleared of tools, the new-to-her TV and couches and coffee table filling up the space. Seeing him in her space—the kindness and concern and the gentleness with how he'd held her, the bright blue eyes and his smile half-hidden by his beard, warm fingers on her cheek, wiping her tears away. Dragging her projects out to safety while she'd stood there like a statue.

She'd known him no time at all, and he'd already become important to her.

Not just because he'd done more for her than any other person, ever—more for her than she'd ever *allowed* anyone to do for her. Just barreling through her walls and barriers, making himself at home inside her heart with how he listened to her blabber on about sharks and wood, how he'd seen that she was struggling when she'd done her level best to stop anyone from noticing.

She could save herself.

But it would have taken more time, more blood and sweat and tears.

And then he'd appeared and paid attention and smiled at her

and kissed her and wiped her tears when it seemed as though she *couldn't* save herself. When she was at the bottom of that deep, dark hole, clinging to the wall with just her fingertips, hands and legs throbbing as she tried to claw her way to the circle of light that seemed so far above her head, he'd been the one to reach into the hole, to offer his hand.

To brace and tug and help her climb the rest of the way out.

Now she was out. Now she had space to live, to breathe, to *think*.

And what she was thinking was that she wasn't going to let the wonderful man who'd given her the opportunity to do so deal with his demons alone.

So, she grabbed her jacket. Her phone. Her keys and her purse.

Then she walked out her front door.

———

It was cold, but she didn't mind.

Not when she had a thick coat and a full belly and a sky full of bright stars.

Charlie was gone for a long time, long enough that she wondered if he was going to come home at all and if she was going to have to sleep on his porch. He had a cozy loveseat sitting in one corner, gray wicker covered with thick white cushions and a plethora of colorful pillows. She could totally get a good night's sleep on that.

Turned out she didn't have to.

Because he pulled into his driveway just after midnight.

The garage door rumbled open just as he slid to a stop, stepping out of his car. He didn't jump when she emerged out of the shadows and began walking toward him, though his shoulders went stiff.

"Hey," she called softly.

His shoulders slumped slightly, whether in relief or in surrender, she didn't know.

"Hey," he said, then slammed the driver's side door and started for the garage. Which was full of boxes. Which explained why he was parking in the driveway rather than inside, and why he had been forced to interact with his ex.

And now her.

A twinge of guilt slid through her.

Especially when she saw the dark circles under his eyes. They'd had an eventful weekend and now she was dragging that out.

He crossed the threshold, started to disappear into the stack of boxes.

She followed, caught his arm. "Charlie, I just—"

"Don't, Kacee."

Not sweetheart. Not Kace. Not warm. Not full of the bright blue summer sky.

It was firm and cold and...she didn't like it.

Nor did she like it when he spun again, dislodging her hand and continuing to walk.

"You didn't hurt me."

A slow rotation, one brow lifted and laced with derision, calling her on that.

"You gripped me too tight for like three seconds," she said, stepping closer, ignoring the dart of pain when he stepped back, putting distance between them. "I called you on it, and you immediately let me go. That was it. Which means it was so *not* a big deal and—"

That was the wrong thing to say.

She knew it the moment the words crossed her lips. Hell, she knew it was the wrong thing the moment the words began to form.

But they were out faster than her common sense could process.

The hurt in his eyes—there and then masked so quickly she

barely saw it—was the worst part. The next was the anger. Then the blankness.

Okay, that was the worst.

Because not once had he looked at her like that.

Like she didn't belong. Like she shouldn't have come into his space, his house, his life.

"That's not what I meant," she began.

Silence.

Then his chin came up. "Look, Kacee. I had a nice time with you, but I'm not in the market for a charity case."

That hurt.

But she had enough of a prickly exterior that she understood he was pushing her away. Protecting himself, maybe protecting her. Either way, he was throwing up all the roadblocks.

However, this was the man who'd saved her.

Saved her cabinet and pulled her out of the dark hole. Made her breathe and think and stare into the sunshine again.

So prickly wouldn't push her away.

Not now. Not ever.

"Right," she said, brushing by him and striding up through the path of boxes. Her hand slapped against the buttons mounted near the front, and she didn't stop to watch the garage door begin to close. Instead, she reached for the knob, pushed open the wooden panel, and then walked into Charlie's kitchen.

The door swung shut behind her.

But only for a second.

And by the time it opened again, Charlie storming into the house, she already had two glasses out, a bottle of tequila on the counter, and was pouring them shots.

"This isn't—"

"You know my ex stole from me," she said, then downed her glass in one go. "But it wasn't just my tools and my money. He stole everything. Everything from my saws to my wood stores to the cheap paintings on my wall. He even stole my shampoo and conditioner. My toothpaste. My truck. And the money out of my savings and checking accounts." She shoved his glass at him, went back to the bottle of tequila and refilled her glass. "Things had been tight for me since I'd bought the house, but I was making progress on the mortgage, could afford to do things for fun, to have all the streaming things. Then he took off and sold my shit, and things were suddenly so tight that I might as well have been trying to fit myself into a pair of leather pants."

She moved to him again, put a finger under the bottom of the glass, lightly tipped it up.

He just stared at her.

So, she gave him two for the price of one.

"I was the misfit," she said. "Always. From the time I entered the system—young enough that I don't remember anything of my mom except that the color of her hair"—she tugged at her own ponytail—"was like mine. Anything else of hers gone, replaced by the years after that, shuffled around foster home after foster home, losing any sense of myself, my belongings, my...any sense of *me*," she finished quietly. And then gulped again. "I got out at sixteen. I worked and rented a room, and I was determined that I'd work my ass off until I had a place where I felt like I was home." She took a breath. "And when I bought my house, I had found it, and then it was almost ripped away," she went on, "all because I chose the wrong man, the wrong person to trust."

His knuckles were white, standing out sharply against his skin as he gripped the glass tightly.

"But you know what tonight taught me? What last night did?" She marched over to the bottle, filled and drank again, then moved back to him, pouring a splash into his glass, just for good measure. "It made me realize that home wasn't so much a place as it is a feeling. Of belonging. Of warmth and people that don't make me feel like I'm trash. People who barrel through my walls." She smiled, stepped close enough to smell the spice of his scent, to be able to stare into those bright blue eyes. "Or people who give me the motivation to tear them down." She sipped, the burn joining the pleasant heat in her stomach, inching up her throat.

"Because you gave me what I was searching for," she whispered. "And it wasn't something I'm going to get from a mortgage payment. It was something I was too scared to acknowledge that I wanted because if I did, if I wanted you, if I wanted friends, a family that I built, they might see..." A sigh. "They might—no they *would* see and they would find me lacking. They would leave or send me away and—"

Here her voice broke and she was forced to sip again, to use that burn down her esophagus to settle herself.

"No, I knew they would send me away. Like my mother had. Like all those foster homes did. Or they would leave me and I would be alone again and—"

His fingers came to her cheek, brushed gently. "Sweetheart," he whispered.

With warmth in those bright blue summer sky eyes.

"I wanted," she whispered. "But all the same, I was scared of that want. So, I didn't make it easy for people to be friends with me, and I sure as shit didn't make it easy to date me. Especially after—"

His palm flattened against her cheek, a soft touch that had her eyes stinging, had her finishing the words that were pinging around in her head, that needed to come out. Because he needed to know.

"But with you... *You,* I wanted more than the fear, the walls, the pushing away. *You,* I accepted that I would take whatever scraps you would toss my way—"

"Sweetheart."

She covered his palm with her own, kept going. "Because what you made me feel was so big and important and wonderful that even though it would hurt like hell when it was over, when you left—because, of course, you would leave me—"

"*Sweetheart.*"

"I knew a day would come when it would happen and I didn't care. I wanted it anyway. I wanted *you* anyway."

"Kacee. Baby. Stop talking."

She didn't. Just leaned closer and rose on tiptoe so their gazes were aligned head-on. "So yeah, your grip on me was too tight. But, it wasn't anger and it wasn't that you were trying to hurt me." Her voice dropped. "And I know that it wasn't...because you stopped immediately when I told you, because you were horrified when you realized that whatever fucked up demons are in your head—and I know they're not you and that they're fucked up because I have demons, too, and my demons love to hop aboard the fucked up merry-go-round at the worst possible time, too, and I know it was them spinning around like maniacal toddlers in your head that caused your hands to tighten and that the tightening has nothing to do with the real Charlie I know.

"The real Charlie brought me popcorn and drills and rescued my livelihood. The real Charlie tried to help with the sheetrock and was determined to keep going, even when he tried to electrocute himself but didn't get all huffy when I sent him off to polish tools because it was safer. The real Charlie is warm and sweet and fucking awesome and convinced me to go on a date with him and let him in when I was determined to not let *anyone* in, and I'm not going to ask you to tell me what your demons are. That's not fair, even if they are maniacal toddlers hopped up on cotton candy and demanding to have ladybugs painted on their cheeks. They're your demons—and they might be assholes like tiny sugar-high humans, but they're yours to share or not—though, of course, I hope that you *do* share them and—"

Here she broke off, breathing hard, mostly due to the fact that spouting that many words was a lot of cardio—and this was coming from a person who twerked in a giant gold poop-shaped costume on the regular and hauled around wood and cabinets the rest of her time (a.k.a. was in decent shape).

But it was also because she'd just laid it all out there.

Wide and open, bared right down to the bone.

It was terrifying and necessary, and even the two-and-a-half shots of tequila didn't quite take the edge off.

Half because when she broke off, huffing and puffing and

trying desperately to suck in air so she could finish verbal vomiting *all* the words floating around her brain and didn't immediately begin up again, Charlie dropped his glass onto the counter, sending tequila sloshing over the edge.

She gaped at the waste of perfectly good alcohol.

But only for a minute.

Because then he plucked the glass out of her hand, dropping *it* onto the counter next to his, sloshing *her* perfectly good alcohol over the rim and onto the gray speckled granite.

She stared at it.

But only for a second.

Because then his hand joined the one currently cupping—and gently stroking, now that she realized it—her cheek, and he murmured, "Sweetheart."

Her lips parted.

His eyes blazed, hotter than the sun.

Then he bent and kissed her.

Twenty-One

CHARLIE

Slow, he thought. *Slow*.

But the moment his lips hit Kacee's, his world shrank again. He didn't worry about the tequila spilled over the counter, no doubt dripping down the front of the cabinets, didn't think about how miserable he'd been feeling the last few hours.

He just felt...Kacee.

Her body and tongue. Her skin and hands.

Her words wrapped around him like the warmest, softest blanket on the planet

When she slipped her hand from beneath his and reached for the hem of his T-shirt, yanking it up, he didn't stop her. Though it was difficult to tear his mouth from hers, he managed for the fraction of a second it took to tear the cotton free of his body, tossing it to the ground and then going right back to kissing her.

She tasted...of Kacee.

Of home and right and perfect for him.

Then she reached down and tugged at the button on his jeans, keeping their mouths locked together, but those strong and slightly calloused hands making short work of the fastening, deftly unzipping.

He groaned when her hand dove inside his boxer briefs, when it cupped him boldly, fingers wrapping tight, so fucking tight that he felt as though he might explode right then and there, especially where she gripped and then stroked, fingers dipping up and over the head of him, finding the sensitive spot right at the tip that had stars flashing behind his eyes, his mouth tearing from hers, a growl tearing free of his throat.

He dipped down and found her neck, thanking every god out there that she managed to keep hold of him, to continue stroking even as he whipped her shirt off, leaving it to hang from the arm whose hand was shoved down his pants like a bizarre bracelet, one that was joined by her bra when he unclasped it and then allowed it to join in with the accessorizing. Her breasts were...so much better up close than across a changing room, rosy tipped and heavy, nipples beading tightly and calling for his mouth.

So, he bent and sucked one deep, her moan in response sliding down his spine, arrowing straight beneath those tight little and very talented fingers, squeezing his cock even more tightly than she was gripping it.

More stars.

More...

He didn't fucking know. The only thing he *did* understand was that standing there kissing her wasn't nearly enough. He needed them naked. He needed to be inside and thrusting deep. He needed to—

Lifting her, he spun and set her on the counter, dislodging her hand, which was a crime against fucking nature, but because it was for the greater good, he survived. Then shoved her pants down, yanked his wallet out of his own before shoving *them* down. Tearing through the worn leather to find the emergency condom inside, thank fuck finding it and finding it fast. Then dropping his wallet to the floor, ripping the packet open with his teeth, and sheathing it over his cock.

"Now," she ordered.

And he wanted that. Wanted it so much that he was ready to thrust home and deep and get lost in oblivion.

But he had to make sure she was ready, that she was wet and aching and—

He slid his fingers up her thigh, dipped into the folds of her pussy. Fuck yes, she was wet. He traced through her liquid heat, slid one finger deep.

She hissed out a breath. "Inside me," she demanded, throwing her head back, her hips already working against his finger.

That was so fucking pretty, so goddamned sexy, that he decided he needed to make her come first, to break apart on his fingers, maybe his mouth. Or both. Most definitely both. So, he pressed another finger in, curling them up, spreading them wide. Her lips parted on a moan, one that he had to taste, so he leaned in, took her mouth.

Tasted her sweetness on his tongue.

Swallowed her cries of pleasure.

Thrust slow and steady and deep, until she was absolutely drenched and dripping around him, until her thighs shook and her pussy convulsed and she finally had to break her mouth free from his, crying out his name.

Red hazed the edges of his vision, but he would never forget the sight of those hazel eyes darkening, turning a molten gold that was swirled with brown and green. Her lips, swollen and red from his mouth. The feel of her fingers gripping his hair tight enough to sting, but it was the best bite of pain he'd ever experienced.

And then he wanted to experience it all over again.

To taste her on his tongue. To hear her call out his name. To watch those hazel eyes grow languid and fuzzy.

So, he started to kneel between her spread thighs.

Her fingers tightening was the only warning he had before she was pushing him back, taking him to the floor. A moment later, she was on top of him, her breasts hanging in front of his face, distracting him from his plans because his hands went there, covering the warm flesh, thumbs dragging over the pink tips.

She gasped...and sank down onto the hard length of him.

Tight.

Hot.

Her wet gathering around the root of his cock, settling onto his skin, pooling between them in sounds that should have been obscene, but instead were perfect, were intoxicating. *He* did that to her. *He* had her so wet that she was dripping around him. *He* had her so turned on that one slide and he was home and deep and—

She started moving.

He groaned, head dropping back to the tile and the pure bliss of it.

But only for a moment. Because then he knew he didn't want to miss a second of this. He wanted it imprinted in his mind forever. Every touch and moan and soft hitch of her breath. The way her breasts swung and bounced, demanding his hands, his fingers and thumbs circling her nipples, pinching and rolling and knowing he found exactly the right touch when her rhythm faltered, when she rode him harder and deeper.

"That's it, sweetheart," he murmured, arching up to take one of her nipples in his mouth, sucking it deeply. "Take me deep, baby. Fuck me harder."

"Oh, shit," she whispered, her hips canting and he slid in deeper, hit a spot that had her pussy clenching around him. "Oh, fuck." Her head dropped forward and she moaned, her rhythm faltering.

Keeping his mouth on her breast, he gripped her hips, helping her when she slowed, guiding her to that peak, her whispered, "Oh, shits" and, "Oh, fucks" a constant litany. One that had him sliding closer and closer to the precipice, especially when her pussy began to clench around him, when her litany broke off into moans and hisses of breath and—finally—thank God *finally*—a long, deep groan, her pussy convulsing, her arms giving way as she collapsed on top of him.

Rolling them, he thrust into her. Once, twice—

And gone.

Pleasure exploding, ripping through him, engulfing him, and he pounded into her, moved through the climax, each stroke sliding them a few inches across the floor until he had to brace his hands on the cabinets so he didn't fuck her into them—or maybe *through* them.

Then he was coming to with the sense that it had been long minutes, or maybe hours, maybe years or centuries later because he was naked and on the tile, holding her tightly, his knees aching, his body cold, his gaze catching on the mess of his kitchen. The world could have stood still again, years could have flown by, nothing mattered in that moment except for this woman and what she'd shared, how she felt, how she made *him* feel.

How she was looking up at him.

"Kacee," he murmured.

Her smile was beautiful—gentle and sweet and so fucking beautiful that it took his breath away. He stroked his hand up her side, loving the way her lips parted slightly, goose bumps prickled to life on her skin.

She was silk and satin, and he wanted to touch her forever.

Then his hip twinged, and he remembered where they were.

On the floor. Cold and hard and...when was the last time he'd cleaned it? Fuck. And she had goose bumps. She had goose bumps because he was lying there on top of her with her head two inches from the kitchen cabinets, on the hard and probably dirty floor, and—

Fingers on his cheek.

"This is why I told you to drink the tequila," she murmured, wrapping her arms around him and tugging him down so he was more firmly on top of her.

"What?" he asked, shifting his weight so he wasn't crushing her.

"You're spiraling," she said. "Tequila helps to prevent that." A beat. "Speaking from the experience of being a woman who just puked her guts out with tequila courage."

He slid his palms beneath her, shifting her and bringing them both to their feet. Another movement and he had her in his arms, was walking to his bedroom—through his bedroom—and set her on the bathroom counter. He cranked on the shower, took care of the condom, then turned back to face her, mouth opening to say...something.

Who knew what?

But she'd given him a lot, and he felt like he needed to say *something,* but the thought of admitting what had happened between him and Ji-Ho, the thought of admitting that he still felt pain from not being what his parents expected when he was a grown-ass fucking man, thought of—

Fingers on his cheek.

"I meant what I said earlier," she whispered. "I shared because I wanted you to know, and I was ready to. But I don't need you to give me something you're not ready to."

"I—"

She hopped down from the counter, traced a hand down his chest. "You know what else I think?"

He shook his head.

"I think that I hope you're into shower sex."

That choking shame dissipated.

He smiled.

Fuck yeah, he was into shower sex.

So much so that he scooped her up, stepped into the stall, and with the water sluicing over their skin, he slanted his mouth to hers.

Twenty-Two

KACEE

A phone ringing distantly had her lids dragging open.

A heavy arm draped over her middle, a warm chest pressed to her back. Spice in her nose. Stubble catching on her hair, rasping against her skin when the ringing cut off and then began again. Then a soft sigh, that arm tightening, and he nuzzled her throat, drawing her closer.

His lips pressed lightly before he released her and slipped out of bed, footsteps padding across the carpet and then disappearing into the hall.

She sighed and buried her face in the pillow, muscles that had been long unused were deliciously sore, and since shower sex had led to bed sex, and all the sex had begun late at night, which meant that all the sex had finished very early in the morning.

And it was still dark outside.

Which meant it was still very early in the morning.

So, all she wanted to do was snuggle down into the soft and cuddly blankets on the soft and cuddly pillows on the soft and cuddly mattress.

So she did.

Her eyes had just slid closed, sleep creeping back up when she felt the mattress depress at her waist, gentle fingers tracing along her arm and pushing back her hair, curving around the shell of her ear. "Hey, sweetheart."

"No," she mumbled, loving the touch, but not wanting reality to intrude on all that soft and cuddly.

A soft chuckle that was almost as good as all the soft and cuddly beneath and surrounding her.

"Grr," she muttered, burrowing in and hating that she liked that chuckle, that it was pulling her from being lazy and cuddled in, but also not hating it because it was pulling her into the reality that was Charlie sitting next to her on the bed looking all rumpled and sleepy and stroking her cheek.

He laughed again, and it rumbled down her spine, settled between her thighs.

Which he knew, the stink.

Based on the heat entering his eyes, the way his fingers flexed on her cheek. "Like that look, sweetheart, but your cell has rung about five times, so I think you'd better answer it."

"My phone—"

She took it from him, checked the screen.

Jimmy.

Fuck.

Fuck.

The soccer games.

"LoLo and Carrie!" She shot up and tossed the covers back, swiping at the screen and quickly calling Jimmy back.

He picked up on the first ring.

"Where are you, Kace?" he asked, sounding worried. "The lights are on, and I knocked, and you're not answering the door."

"I'm...um..."

"I thought we were picking you up."

"I just—" She cleared her throat, got it together. "I had a late night and stayed over at a friend's."

Silence.

Then, "A friend's?"

Her gaze went to Charlie's, and his face was gentle, his eyes on hers equally so. Except, there was heat there, too. Heat that reminded her of the shower sex and the kitchen sex and the bed sex and...the rest of the mental list she had been making of all the other places she wanted to fuck Charlie (wall, stairs, on top of those boxes in his garage, in the front seat of his car, the hot tub she spied out the window, the vanity, the kitchen counter, the kitchen table, the kitchen refrigerator—was there any such thing as a kitchen fridge? Those two things went hand in hand, she supposed. Well, unless one had a *garage* fridge).

"Kacee?"

"Jimmy—"

"A friend's?" he repeated.

"Yes," she murmured. But then Charlie trailed the backs of his fingers over her cheek and she found herself telling Jimmy the rest of it. "A friend and more," she whispered. "He's great."

Bright blue summer sky.

Sunlight on her skin.

"*He's?*"

She smiled. "Yes, Jimmy. *He's* great."

"Well, is *he* going to be driving you to the soccer game? Because LoLo and I need to get a move on so we're not late."

"He doesn't need to drive me to the soccer game," she said. "I can drive myself, same as I told you before, Jimmy." She'd rent a car. Yes, it was last minute. But she would make it work. She *had* to. "I'll be there for kickoff."

She heard footsteps and a door opening and closing, his phone clicking and presumably connecting over onto the Bluetooth of the car. "Kacee—"

"I'm hanging up now, Jimmy. Me and my chair will be there in time for the game—"

"And donuts!" LoLo cried, her little voice punctuating the speaker of her cell in that way that only kids' voices could.

"With donuts," she confirmed. "Okay," she added after LoLo finished cheering. "See you guys in an hour and a half."

They said goodbye, she hung up, and then she started to push up from the bed.

Charlie caught her hand, tugged her against him. Her breath caught, all that spicy scent filling her nose, all those strong muscles pressed so tightly to her. His breath warm in her ear when he said, "We're going to watch some soccer?"

───────

"Take it, LoLo!" Charlie yelled. "That's it, you got it!"

She looked up at the man she was quickly thinking of as her own—and not temporarily either. She was thinking of him as hers in a way that was permanent, in a way that would give her that family, that sense of belonging, that sense of home forever. He was wearing a hooded sweatshirt, jeans that were just tight enough to show off the strength of his thighs, a pair of leather boots whose toes were now dotted with the condensation from the grass.

His breath condensed—the cheers turning into puffs of white —but the cold didn't seem to bother him.

He was focused on the game—completely focused in that way that made Kacee feel so special when he listened to her prattle on about wood joints and sharks cruising to Guadalupe Island. LoLo had darted over to them when they'd first arrived, eyes going wide with pleasure when she'd spotted the box of donuts in Charlie's arms.

It was a big box because he'd bought—yes, *he'd* bought (and totally ignored her argument that she was the one paying)—the girls a cornucopia of deliciousness. Sprinkles and icing, every variety that had been in the case. Probably enough of the fried circles of yumminess for six soccer teams, but then again, the girls would be working hard and she'd seen LoLo put away a lot of sweet carbs. Her bet was on them destroying that box.

And if they didn't, she was going to have donuts for breakfast, lunch, and dinner.

"Yes," he cheered as LoLo carried the ball up the field, getting close to their opponent's goal. "That's it! Keep going! You got it. *Yes!!*" he straight-up yelled at the top of his lungs when LoLo shot and the ball went into the net, jumping up and down in the air and whooping like a loon.

Maddy, who was cheering herself—Carrie beside her bouncing on her toes and clapping as loud as her little hands could—glanced up and met Kacee's eyes, mouthing, "I like him."

Jimmy was on her other side, clapping loudly (and his grown-up hands could clap much louder Carrie's), and when she turned from the field and caught his eye, she found that he had a begrudging smile on his face.

Probably because he'd pegged her *friend,* who was great, and how deep she was in for him all in an instant, and had immediately gone fully into Protective Dad Mode.

Complete with the narrowed eyes, assessing looks (cough, glares), and the tight handshake.

Charlie had let the Protective Dad trifecta roll off his shoulders, endured the brutal handshake with nary a blink, and then given LoLo a high-five, Carrie a bag of donut holes, and had turned his full attention to the game.

Not resentful that he'd been pulled out of bed, not grumbling because it was cold and he was watching grade school kids play soccer.

Fully invested in it.

Even if she was less so because *she* was cold, because she wasn't much of a soccer fan, and because as much as she loved LoLo, she'd rather be in bed actively checking off her sexual to-do list with Charlie.

Partly because she would be warm.

Yeah, the orgasms would be good.

But the warmth part was sounding really good right about then, especially when she was turning into a human Popsicle.

She shivered, and even though Charlie was standing a few feet away from her, it appeared that he'd sensed it. He turned, slipped an arm around her shoulders, and tugged her close to him, her front to his side, rubbing his hand up and down her back, kissing the top of her head. "Want my jacket, sweetheart?" he asked, the words rumbling down to her ear.

Considering she was currently wrapped up in his strong arms, experiencing his special brand of warmth all without them missing a moment of the game, surrounded by him, held by him, his care obvious.

She didn't have to ask or beg or demand it.

She just needed to be there to accept it.

"I'm good," she murmured. "I'm good as long as you're holding me."

A gentle stroke on her back. A soft kiss to her hair. His hold tightening. "I can do that, baby."

And he did.

He held her as she slowly unfroze from Popsicle status, held her as LoLo made an awesome pass and they both whooped with joy. He held her until he'd needed to disseminate donuts, until they'd recapped the game with LoLo, until they chatted and small talked and Jimmy moved from Protective Dad Mode to Slightly Suspicious Dad Mode.

Which she considered a victory, so they said their goodbyes and drove the hour home, fully thinking that they'd go their own ways, that she'd work for a few hours, pick up a rental, and then drive to Carrie's game.

But Charlie had driven to her house, parked in her driveway.

And then he'd walked into her house and whipped up strawberry waffles with homemade whipped cream.

Like it was the easiest thing in the world, like they hadn't gorged themselves on leftover donuts (though not as many as she'd expected, mainly because little girls could gorge *themselves* on donuts—albeit not leftover ones).

Like it was the simplest thing ever to just whip up a meal in her kitchen.

To sit down across from her.

To make that sense of belonging grow and settle and not feel like it was going to be ripped away.

Then he'd packed sandwiches for their second road trip of the day, grabbed the second box of donuts for Carrie's team, and stowed both in the trunk.

And after that, they watched Carrie's team win regionals.

And celebrated with sprinkles and frosting and Charlie's special brand of cheers.

Twenty-Three

CHARLIE

The weekend had been a lot.

Wonderful and amazing with the smallest dash of drama (and self-doubt, though he was doing his best to erase that slip-up from his mind).

The point was, he'd finally gotten into Kacee—

And no, he didn't mean like *that*, though the *like that* had been fucking incredible.

He just...the hand she'd been holding up had dropped to her side, and she had let him in, and—

He wasn't prepared.

For his breath to be stolen.

By the slam into the wall in the parking garage.

His head cracked against the wall, stars flashing behind his eyes, pain radiating down his spine. Then Ji-Ho was in his face. "What the fuck are you playing at, Charlie?"

Cold, sharp words. Even colder, semi-robotic eyes. Fingers digging into his arm.

"Let me go."

It was a demand, but it wasn't a strong one. Or at least not one strong enough to penetrate the barbed exterior of his ex. Ji-Ho didn't loosen his grip, just leaned closer, heat puffing on Charlie's face. "Fuck you."

And *that* was trailed by spit.

"You know," he said. "I don't know what I ever saw in us, why I fought for us." They'd had so few good times. He'd just been so used to hell, to rolling in shit that he hadn't realized what good times were. The bastardized version he'd had with Ji-Ho was nothing like what he'd had with Kacee this past weekend.

One weekend and he already had more good memories than in almost a year with Ji-Ho.

A year when he'd allowed himself to be torn down and torn apart and shredded into little pieces.

"You fought for *me,*" Ji-Ho spat.

He had.

Shame thick in his throat, burning down, flame licking through his gut.

"You love *me.*"

Loved. And maybe not that. Because the feelings were all so twisted together, so thick and murky and unclear. No, not love— or at least not of the healthy variety.

"No, Ji-Ho," he said, shoving his ex away, shoving the shame down, breaking the hold Ji-Ho had on him, even though that fucking hurt because the bastard didn't let go easily. "I don't love you. I would be fucking happy to never *ever* see you in my life again." A flash of anger. "But we work together. We need to get along, and that means you can't do this. So, unless it's work-related, I don't want you around me. And if you do this again, I'll—"

That flash again.

Only this time, it was accompanied by a flash of movement, one that took Charlie by surprise, and one that found his head whipping against that wall again.

More pain.

More stars.

"You'll do *what?*" Ji-Ho snapped, in his face again with all the spit and all the hissing and all the fury of a man who had no fucking clue that he was the one who was in the wrong.

But the shame stayed buried. Because Charlie shoved him away again. Faster this time. Easier and with less hesitation. Finally reacting. Finally not frozen and pathetic. He straightened his shoulders, took a step for the door that would lead out of the parking garage and to the bank of elevators that he'd take up to his floor. "I'll report you to HR," he said, "and I'll—"

Ji-Ho laughed.

It was terrible, and that derision sliced through any strength he'd managed to cobble together, sliced him to the quick, allowed that shame to leak out again. His footsteps faltered, bile burned—

"Is everything okay?"

That shame magnified, swallowing him up when he saw Kelsey Scott coming his way. When he saw his *boss* walking toward them, concern on her face.

While in the middle of an ugly confrontation with his ex.

More shame, a bitter wave of it splashing over him. No, not a wave. A tsunami of it, crashing down, battering him against rocks and debris, shoving him under, choking him, *drowning* him.

He was battling that, trying to keep his head above water, so he nearly missed it, missed the rapid transformation that Ji-Ho underwent—from cruel bully to suave, confident businessman.

"Kelsey," he said, the rage erased, the charm turned on. "Charlie and I were just having a discussion about the code for the Prometheus project."

Kels's gaze caught on Charlie's, her brown eyes holding some emotion he couldn't decipher before she turned to Ji-Ho. "And why were you *discussing* the code with Charlie when I explicitly told you that I was the lead on this project and that any and all communication would go directly through me? Do you get me, Ji-Ho?"

Surprise froze that shame in place.

Both at the sharpness that had entered Kels's tone (yeah, she was his boss, but they'd always worked like equals on their team, to see her step into intense boss mode was surprising) and Ji-Ho's reaction to it (he went blank, totally and utterly blank, and Ji-Ho wasn't a man to go blank, to stare in silence, his mouth agape, especially when he'd been reprimanded).

Charlie had expected rage at Kelsey's admonishment.

He hadn't expected Ji-Ho to stand there without a retort.

And he didn't have time to see if that retort was still coming, just had been delayed in the process, because Kelsey wound her arm through his, tugged him toward the elevators. "Come on," she said. "I wanted to talk to you about the roll-out schedule."

He let her lead him to the bank of elevators and onto one of the cars.

Kels hit the button for their floor, and immediately she started talking about the roll-out schedule—and thankfully not about the fact that she'd stumbled upon the confrontation between him and Ji-Ho.

But as the metal doors began to close, he glanced back.

Glanced back and saw Ji-Ho still standing there.

The blank was gone.

Rage had made its delayed appearance.

And it was written all over Ji-Ho's face.

———

Throat clearing jarred him out of his hard-won work headspace.

Hard-won for obvious reasons.

Kels had talked about that roll-out until they reached their floor, and as they walked out, after he'd somehow managed to participate in the conversation, he'd thought he'd faked it well enough, thought he would escape any probing questions.

And he did for a few minutes, anyway.

Until he'd started to turn for his desk and she caught his arm. "Charlie?"

He'd halted, dread pooling. "Yeah, Kels?"

"You'll let me know if you're not good?"

Those cracks had begun widening, shame leaking out. Then he'd nodded. "Yeah, I will."

So, it wasn't a surprise that it had taken a while for him to focus on the actual shit he needed to get done and not on the shit his ex had heaped onto his Monday morning after a great weekend, reminding him again that he'd been a pathetic hapless weakling for far too long.

The throat-clearing penetrated again, and he tugged off his headphones as he glanced up and saw—

"Scar!" he exclaimed, setting them on his desk. "What are you doing here?"

She rounded his workstation, bent and kissed him on the cheek. "I gave you one full day without asking a million questions. "Why do you think that I'm here?"

"Kacee," he said.

She grinned. "Of course, it's about Kacee." A beat. "Oh, and also about taking my favorite brother to lunch."

It was a joke, but she knew they both felt the same pulse of pain. It arched across the look they shared, embedded itself in his heart, that missing of their favorite brother, the hole Heath had left behind.

"You can have two favorite brothers," he said gently.

"Right," she whispered.

He tugged her ponytail. "Exactly right, and you know it. Just like you know that Heath would have said the same thing."

"Yeah." More whispering. "He would have."

"Same as he'd tell me that I needed to feed you so you wouldn't have the afternoon tummy rumbles."

Her smile was wide, and the sad left her eyes. "God, I'd forgotten about that. How many peanut butter sandwiches did he make us for breakfast, lunch, and dinner?"

"Because he couldn't make anything else?" he asked. And seriously, their parents had been utter shit. He remembered more than one time when his parents had gone out of town and left them at home where the only thing to eat was a half-stale loaf of bread and a jar of peanut butter with only a few tablespoons left in it.

Left at home to fend for themselves at far too young of an age —hell, they couldn't have been more than six and eight, and Heath must have been twelve. But his brother had never made it scary, even though there was no way they should have been left alone for days at a time.

A nod. "Well, that, and because there wasn't anything else."

He wrapped his arm around her waist. "Too many times." He squeezed. "We were lucky to have him."

Her head dropped to his shoulder. "Yes, we were." A sigh. "I miss him," she murmured. "A lot." Her head lifted, eyes hitting his. "But I really would be okay never *ever* eating another peanut butter sandwich again."

Laughing, he wove his arm through hers, led her to the elevator. "I think I can arrange something better."

"Molly's?" she asked hopefully.

"And *that's* why you're my favorite sister." Molly's was the best bakery in town and they had much better sandwiches than stale bread and a few scraped-together tablespoons of peanut butter. Plus, they had cookies.

"You're *only* sister."

He shrugged. "Same difference."

They stepped onto the elevator, hit the button for the garage. "And while we're there," she said, clearly fishing, "you can pick up Kacee's favorite type of cookie."

He bopped her on the nose. "Clever." A beat. "But you know that we're new enough that I don't yet know her favorite cookie."

"It's cinnamon sugar," she stage-whispered, rising on tiptoe and bopping *him* on the nose.

"See?"

The doors opened and they walked off, Scar leading him to her car. "See what?"

He wound his arm through hers, led her to *his* car. "See, that's why you're my favorite sister."

"*Only* sister."

"Same difference."

Her laughter trailed him all the way to Molly's.

And it was the second greatest sound in the world—to hear the evidence of his sister's happiness.

Second because the only thing that trumped it was Kacee's.

Which was why he bought a dozen cinnamon cookies.

Twenty-Four

KACEE

"Oh fuck," she breathed as he slid in deep.

Not slowly. Not gently. Just in one rough stroke that jolted her against the wall. A picture frame—new and hung on her wall after Charlie had found the pictures that her ex had left behind—rattled.

A week ago, he'd shown up with the frames and had filled them all with pictures and hung them all while she'd been finishing up a project in the garage. She'd come in to the smell of homemade pasta sauce boiling on the stove, homemade ravioli waiting and ready to be cooked, and...her walls full of the photographs.

Ones she'd taken with an old disposable camera a foster mom had given her and saved up her nickels and pennies and dimes and quarters to develop. Others she'd printed semi-pixelated from an ancient iPhone she'd had for well beyond its recommended shelf life. A few from recent trips, from those before her life had taken its turn.

And one of them together, a month before, sitting on the floor surrounded by the Gold kiddos. He had his arm around her. She had her head on his shoulder. They weren't looking at the camera. She hadn't even *known* there was a camera. Instead, they were looking at each other, her head tilted, staring up at him as he stared down at her.

Both of them smiling. Naturally.

And she was happy in it.

And she was *in* it.

All of her other pictures were of special places and things. None were of her. None had her smiling like *that*.

He thrust again, and she forgot about the pictures and her smiling in that one. She forgot about the month with Charlie that kept getting better and better. She forgot about falling asleep in his bed or hers every night. She forgot about what it was like to be able to breathe again because she had a full fridge and furniture and projects being completed.

Because Charlie helped her in the evenings.

He was a good assistant. He was an even better cook.

And...he was an even better *better* boyfriend.

He shifted, hit a spot that should have been criminal, and her head flew back, colliding with the wall. More pictures rattled, and his hand slid between her and the sheetrock.

Protecting her.

Even as he fucked her. Hard.

"Come on, baby," he ordered, rolling his hips and grinding deep.

Oh *fuck*. God, that was the spot. That was. Just. The. *Right*. Spot.

"Charlie," she breathed.

"Come, sweetheart," he growled, hips moving faster, thrusting deeper, hitting that spot—hitting that glorious *fucking* spot. "Come on my cock and do it. *Now*."

"I—" She arched against him, pressing down, needing him in, needing all of him, needing—

"Now, baby." More orders, still thrusting and grinding. One

hand at her hip angling her so she could take him deeper, the other behind her head.

Protecting and consuming.

Caring and driving her higher.

It was glorious and it was too much and it wasn't enough and she was overwhelmed because she couldn't do it—she just couldn't—

"Kacee," he said, still growling as he moved in her.

"I can't," she moaned.

That hand at her hip flexed, and in one fluid movement he pulled out, flipped her around. He bent her at the waist and she barely had time to brace her hands against the wall before he was pushing into her again. The angle was intense, stretching her wide, but he showed no mercy, setting a rhythm that had her immediately losing her breath. Then her voice as his fingers found her clit. She screamed. Literally screamed. Because he wasn't showing mercy there either. His circles were firm and persistent. "God, I love how fucking wet you are." He nipped at her throat, fingers digging into her hips. Cock still driving deep. Body curved around hers. Hot breath on her skin. "I love the way you feel clasped around my cock."

His hands slid up, cupped her breasts, fingers rolling her nipples, thumbs brushing over the tops of the hard and aching buds, arcing pleasure through her body. It swelled within her, so big and intense that it felt like it was going to consume her, overwhelm her, burn her to ash.

"Come, sweetheart," he ordered again, teeth finding the top of her ear.

A bolt of pain. A swell of pleasure.

Ash and woman. Herself and completely lost.

She moaned, bucking against him, pressing back, taking him deeper and harder and—

"Oh God."

"Yeah, baby," he growled. "That's it. You take what I'm giving. You take what you want." His hands left her breasts and he bent over her, dragging them up her arms, linking their fingers together.

She jolted.

That angle. The feel of her wrapped around him. So full and deep and hard.

"Charlie," she whispered.

"Yes, sweetheart. You take it."

"I—"

One stroke. Another. *Another.*

He didn't stop.

Not even when she jolted again. Not even when more tension expanded inside her. A balloon being pumped full of helium, expanding more and more by the second until...

Pop.

All that tension disappeared in an explosion that took her hearing, her eyesight, that reduced her to a single nerve...that was filled with pleasure and nothing else.

Her knees gave way.

He banded an arm around her waist, holding her upright, keeping her on her feet as he thrust, once, twice, a handful more times.

His groan hit her ears as her hearing distantly returned.

His body jerked and shuddered and still he protected her, kept her safe, even as he was overwhelmed by his own pleasure.

And then he went still.

His lips pressed to her throat. His free hand smoothed gently down her hair.

And...she fell.

Deep.

Those emotions bubbled within her, expanding faster than that balloon of pleasure, popping rapidly, filling every cell, curling around every strand of DNA. They seared themselves right into her soul.

But for once in her life when the connection deepened between her and another person, when the bond tightened, when she hoped for a future that would never *ever* end, what Kacee felt wasn't fear.

It was love.

And she'd spent her lifetime hiding from it, hiding from her need for it, from the pain it would leave when it ceased to exist.

But right then, right at that moment, she knew she needed to tell him.

"Charlie?" He straightened, taking her with him, lifting her gently into his arms and carrying her to her bedroom. He had to sidestep one picture frame that had been fucked off the wall along the way, but he did it without missing a beat, and she knew that when he set her on the bed, tugged the covers up and over her, and disappeared back into the hall that he wasn't hitting the kitchen for a midnight snack.

He was hanging the picture back up.

Because he was thoughtful and kind and sweet and had treated her like she was the most important thing in his universe.

Which was why when he walked back into the room, naked and yummy as hell, she found herself blurting, "I love you!"

Or rather, she yelled it.

Straight up yelled it.

And that was probably why he stumbled to a stop, his eyes going wide. "I—" A shake of his head. "What?"

"I love you," she said again, sitting up and holding the sheets to her chest.

His face fell.

There was no other description for it.

Not joy. But...panic?

And he wasn't coming over to the bed, wasn't taking her in his arms and declaring his undying love back.

He was staring at her. Now with the panic tucked away.

"Charlie?" she whispered.

He turned, walked toward their clothes, piled on the floor where he'd cornered her after she'd finished in her workshop for the night, stripping her and then taking her into the shower. He'd given her an orgasm there, too, against the tile, and as she'd come down, she'd breathlessly admitted that she'd been thinking about him fucking her against a wall for a while now.

Which had preceded him turning the shower off by about three seconds, giving them both a cursory wipe with her towels.

Then the wall and that amazing sex.

Then fixing the picture and tucking her into bed.

And now...

"I can't do this," he rasped out, reaching for his underwear and tugging it on. "I *cannot* do this."

Shock had her throat freezing. Then her feet found the floor and she was tugging the blankets up with her, wrapping them around her as she stumbled toward him. "Wh-what?"

His pants were next, and he hopped on one foot and then the other as he yanked them up, rocking from side to side, bumping into her dresser, nearly knocking her things off the top.

She reached him as he was yanking his shirt over his head.

"What are you doing?"

Head popping out whack-a-mole style, he met her stare, and the cold in them took her breath away.

Took *her* away.

Back to that moment, back to the past.

To that crawling, sinking feeling. To knowing that he was going to leave and there wasn't a damned thing she could do about it.

"Don't do this."

He shoved his feet into his shoes, shook his head. "I can't do *this.*"

Needing something on, something that covered her, she grabbed her robe from the back of the door, swapped it for the bedsheets. "Because I love you?"

The panic was creeping back in. "Because I can't do *this.*"

"*This* being us?"

Those summer sky eyes went wide, and when she reached for him, he skittered back several steps.

"Because I love you," she asked again, "or because you love me back and that scares you?"

He froze.

She waited, but when he didn't speak, she did her best to remain calm. "What happened with Ji-Ho?" she asked.

His eyes shuttered. "What happened with my ex doesn't matter."

"Like what happened with *my* ex didn't matter? Like my childhood didn't matter?"

He shook his head, repeated stubbornly. "He doesn't matter."

She stared at him, edging to the door, suddenly hating her promise a month before that she wouldn't push him to talk about his ex, to confide in her those painful memories. If she had, they might not be here. Him acting like a cornered animal while she tried to not panic because he was literally doing the single thing that she feared the most.

The thing she knew he wouldn't do if he wasn't currently spiraling. "He matters," she said softly. "You know he matters because the Charlie that I've known over the last month, the Charlie that brought me popcorn and arranged a Gold supply chain run and held pieces of wood and cooked me homemade ravioli and made love to me like I was the most precious person on this planet wouldn't be getting dressed and running away when I told him how I felt." She swallowed hard as he shook his head, as he turned to the door. "He would be holding me close."

He stepped into the hall.

She followed. "He would be telling me he loved me back because he's spent the last month showing me that. He would be kissing me and that kissing would lead to more and then we would be planning our future, and that future would be something during which I fear he would leave me." She sucked in a breath as he bounded down the stairs, her eyes starting to prickle, fear gathering on her nape. "He wouldn't leave, even if he didn't feel the same because he's not the kind of man to leave without sorting this out, not when he knows what that would do to me."

He'd get to the bottom of the stairs and her words would process. He would snap out of it. He'd confide in her, and they could talk it out, and they could move on and—

He grabbed his jacket.

"Because you know what it did to me," she whispered as he tugged it on, as he shoved his wallet and his keys into his pocket. "Because I told you what it did. Because you found me when I was at the rock bottom of that. Because you knew and—"

Because this wasn't actually happening, right?

This was some horrible multiple-orgasm-induced nightmare and she'd wake up and he would be holding her and—

He yanked open the front door.

"Charlie." It was a plea. "Please." That even more so.

Please close the door.

Please walk back inside.

Please don't do this.

Please don't make her feel this way.

Please...just *don't.*

She saw it in his eyes before he spoke, and the impact of his decision took everything she had inside her to stay on her feet, to not crumple and burst into tears.

"I can't do this," he said.

And fuck, she hated those words.

Almost as much as she hated that she had the urge to beg, that the idea of him walking out, of not having all of the things he'd brought into her life, of not having *him* was shattering.

But even if she *had* given in to that urge, even if she *had* begged, she wouldn't have had an audience.

Because he stepped out onto the porch.

The door slammed.

And then he was gone.

And then...she was alone.

Again.

TWENTY-FIVE

CHARLIE

It had been a week.

One week without Kacee, and one week where he'd gone over that night, gone over it in his head again and again and *again*.

And he didn't know how he could possibly do anything different.

He'd thought he could do it.

He'd thought he could just move on from Ji-Ho and find the value in himself, have a good relationship. But the moment Kacee had told him she loved him, he'd *known*. He'd *known*.

He couldn't be what she needed.

Her declaration had made a cold sweat break out at his spine. He'd wanted to lash out, to push her away and prevent her from getting any closer. He'd wanted to exploit every bit of weakness she'd exposed to him to do that.

He'd wanted to *hurt* her.

Because the last time someone had said they loved him, he'd nearly been destroyed.

And that urge to wound her, to wound that beautiful, amazing woman, had been so intense that he'd nearly done it.

Never would he have forgiven himself for that.

What he'd done was already bad enough.

He would never forgive himself. So, he needed to stay away.

But, fuck, it was hard.

With her so close.

Driving up and seeing the lights on in her garage, knowing that she probably wasn't taking care of herself or eating enough— knowing that it probably wasn't *probably* at all.

Because he'd seen those lights on all night.

Because he'd been up all night.

Every night.

And staring at her house, like a fucking creeper.

Which meant that he was miserable and exhausted and a total fucking mess. Which *meant* that he really hadn't been ready to be at work that morning. A case of the Mondays times a fucking million. Not just because he was tired and a damned disaster.

But because of what he'd found on his porch.

A cabinet.

Simple and gorgeously built. Stained to match his kitchen cabinets perfectly and when opened, it created the ideal surface for rolling out pasta. The drawers below held his various tools, and there were even built-in canisters for flour and semolina.

It was a reminder of what they'd had. And it was also goodbye.

He'd cried.

Then he'd dragged it inside, found that it fit like a glove in the small alcove next to his refrigerator.

And he'd cried again.

But he'd known he was doing the right thing.

Not because he was playing the martyr.

But because he couldn't bring his special brand of messed up to Kacee. He'd drawn her out of her shell. He'd given her something that was good in the form of the team and friendship, and for a bit, he'd given her the good in him.

That wasn't something he was going to ruin.

So, he'd take the cabinet. He'd know that it was goodbye.

And he'd figure out the next steps so that he wouldn't ruin that good he'd given her.

Luckily, Scar was away with the team for a road trip, too busy with the team and her job to notice how much of a fucking mess he was.

Otherwise, his sister would have pegged the disaster he was in a heartbeat and then she'd try to fix it, and...there was nothing to fix.

It was over.

It was on him.

He jabbed at the button on the elevator, knowing that he needed some Molly's. Nothing cured a broken heart better than copious amounts of carbs, butter, and sugar.

"Now that looks like a Desperate for Molly's Run Face," Kels said as she strode up beside him. "Please tell me that you're going to the bakery."

He glanced at her, lifted a brow.

She grinned. "Because that gives me an excuse to go and not have to share my cookies with Tanner." Tanner being her husband —the one who was so in love with her that he would definitely let her eat *all* the cookies if she so much as batted those pretty lashes in his direction.

His other brow joined the first.

"Okay, fine," she muttered. "He's traveling for work"— Tanner was a world-renowned photographer—"and made me promise to not get Molly's without him."

The doors opened and he held them for her so she could step on ahead of him.

"Doesn't this break that promise?"

She grinned up at him. "Nope. This is a necessary work lunch."

"A necessary work lunch you crashed during which we won't talk about work at all?"

"Chatting about all the bad reality TV we're watching is important for work."

He hit the button for the garage and the doors began to close...just as Angie, one of the other engineers on their team, caught them and hopped on. "It's lunchtime and Kelsey is salivating. Please tell me that means we're hitting up Molly's."

Kels gasped in outrage as the doors closed. "I am *not* salivating. I'm just...*anticipating*."

Angie caught his gaze, lifted her brows.

"She's salivating."

A fist-pump. "Hell yes. I don't care why we're going, so long as we're going to Molly's."

"I hope you have room for copious amounts of baked goods."

"I do," Angie said, rubbing her belly. "I *do*."

They rode down and the doors opened to the garage. "Does you two crashing my lunch mean that I'm driving?"

Kels laced her arm through his. "Do we look like two women in need of those copious amounts of baked goods?"

"I'm driving," he said, leading them over to his car. He bleeped the locks, opened the doors for them, and just as he started to get into his seat, he saw it.

Saw the note tucked under his windshield.

And his stomach turned.

His ass had been halfway into his seat, but he stopped, straightened, and yanked out the paper.

Nothing on the outside.

When he opened it, that stomach turning went full ocean churning during a hurricane. Because he recognized the handwriting, even as his brain didn't process the words. Or rather, didn't need to process the words.

Because it would be vitriol.

Designed to make him feel like shit. And considering he had just left the woman he loved, doing the stupid fucking cliché hero-in-a-bad-romance thing—pushing her away to protect her—Charlie didn't need to feel more like shit.

He knew leaving Kacee, knew hurting her like that was stupid.

But he didn't know how to make it better, how to heal the wounds in him, the ones that sought to wound *her*. He didn't know how to stop them from raring forward, and if they exploded to the forefront of his mind when she told him she loved him, then what in the fuck all would he do to her when they fought?

So *so* much worse.

He couldn't be that person to her.

Better to end it now, to set her on the course to something good, to finding someone good for her. Even if it fucking hurt that the someone wasn't him.

Not letting those words penetrate, he crumpled the note, tossed it into the cupholder, and got into the driver's seat. Then sighed and hit the button for the ignition before buckling in.

"You good?" Kels asked.

"Great," he said, backing out, fully aware that he didn't sound great. Not in the least. But before his co-workers—lovely women, but also well-entrenched in the circles of the Gold gossip center—could pounce on his tone. "Did I tell you I found a new show?" he asked. "And one of the cast members has been married eleven times?"

Silence.

Then, "Um, what?"

"Yup," he said. "That being one-dash-one, or ten plus one, equaling *eleven*."

More silence.

Then from the back seat, "Dish, please."

Kels was quiet, but when he glanced over at her, her gaze was on her hands—or maybe the cupholder.

On the *note* in the cupholder.

Shit.

He surreptitiously snagged it, shoving it into the cubby in the door near his feet.

Kels's eyes hit his, and he braced.

But she just smiled, and said, pointing behind her, "I'm with that one in the back seat. I would like you to dish on these eleven marriages, please."

He dished on the show and the eleven marriages.

He got them talking about what they were watching, so much so that he distracted them and paid for lunch (and a few extra baked goods) so they couldn't argue over the bill.

They gave him a hard time about it.

But he pulled his bossy male card and because he'd primed them for distraction with those baked goods and delicious salads and yummy soups and then added in an additional dash of entertaining, putting on the happy-go-lucky mask so they would be laughing over the outrageous reality TV they all loved, so they wouldn't know something was wrong with him, so they wouldn't know he was broken into pieces inside.

It worked.

They laughed and gossiped and theorized about their shows.

They teased Kelsey about breaking her promise to Tanner, joked with Angie about rubbing in the fact that her man, Max, a player on the Gold, couldn't eat the treats she was bringing home.

They took more than the hour and not once during that time did they talk about work.

Which was fine with him.

He needed the distraction.

Because not once during that more than an hour did he forget about the note crumpled in his door.

Not once did he forget that it was precisely the reason he'd given up the best thing in his life.

TWENTY-SIX

KACEE

It was hard to shake her ass like a glittering gold poop when she had a broken heart.

Hard to be excited about throwing T-shirts into the crowd and handing off foam pucks to little kids or moderating a tricycle race on the ice so someone could win a jersey.

But she did it.

And she did it like her life depended on it.

Because maybe it did. Or maybe...it didn't? Or maybe the only thing she knew how to do was to keep dancing and shaking her gold booty. To keep working. To keep hoping that eventually she would feel like herself again—

Or to feel like the woman she'd been when Charlie was around.

No.

That woman was her.

Well, it was *her* minus a boatload of financial and emotional stress. But it was still her, and that was what she needed to remember.

The final buzzer went—the first Gold game she'd worked since they'd been on an extended road trip—and she danced her way down the aisles toward her access leading to the bowels of the arena—slapping hands and doing her best to not take out anyone along the way (her costume could definitely define wide load).

Eventually, though, she made it to the bottom of the stairs without injury and slipped behind the black curtain, walking along the hall and moving toward her changing room.

No Charlie to spray her down.

No Charlie to cop a feel in her room.

No Charlie to smooth back her sweaty hair and tease her about her twerking ability.

Fuck, that made her eyes burn. Especially when she saw Scar was waiting for her, huge grin on her face. All that red hair, the eyes that were so similar to Charlie's. What would Scar do when she found out that Kacee and Charlie were over? Would she still be grinning? Would she still greet Kacee with a hug—followed by a sniff and a fist-pump?

Or would things be strictly professional?

Would Kacee lose—

No. No, she wouldn't.

"The cleaning works!" Scar exclaimed, doing a little dance that sent her glasses sliding down her nose. "It works."

Kacee pushed into her room, waiting until Scar followed her before taking off her head.

Scar took it, hung it on the hook in the cleaning station, then helped Kacee shrug out of the Goldie costume, chattering all the while. "You and Charlie need to come over to my place tomorrow. Kaydon is going to grill some chicken with this awesome rub we found in Chicago, and I'm going to make Brussel sprouts, and then you and I and Charlie can have his chocolate pie while Kaydon drools, but he can't have any since his body is a hockey temple and it's not Cheat Day, and—"

Kacee slipped behind the curtain, peeled off her sweaty

clothes as she listened to Scar talk about all the desserts that Charlie was good at making.

Desserts she wouldn't taste.

"I don't think—"

"Oh," Scar interrupted. "Don't think. Just come over and enjoy. It's the least we can do for barreling into your place and taking over and—"

"Bringing food and furniture and a TV and co-opting the guys into helping me fix my garage?" She belted her robe around her, moved out from behind the curtain and strode to the shower, cranking it on. "I think that the least I could do would be to cook or to take you guys out to dinner."

Scar grinned. "You can do that another time. That time being, of course"—she zipped up the deodorizer and set it running—"a time when I haven't bullied my brother into cooking something delicious."

"Okay," she said. "I'll do it another time. But about tomorrow—"

Scar's face fell. "Oh, no. You have plans?"

"Not exactly," she began. "I just—"

"Oh, you need to work? That's okay," Scar said. "Just come over whenever you're done."

"It's not that," she said. "I mean, I do have work. But as far as tomorrow night, I—"

"We can eat late," Scar went on. "And then we can—"

Fuck.

Five minutes with her friend and she was already having to go here. Here being discussing her failed relationship with her brother. "Scar."

"I have this new board game and it works best with four players and—"

"*Scar.*"

"Oh shoot," she said. "Here you are trying to get into the shower and I'm blabbering your ear off. I'll just step out and—"

"*Scar!*"

Dazed blue eyes. A red ponytail swinging as her friend's head jerked.

But at least she stopped talking.

Which meant that she was able to tell Scar the truth. Oh, joy. Just exactly what she wanted to do.

The silence stretched for a moment, and then Kacee gave that truth. "Charlie and I broke up."

"*What?*"

"We broke up, Scar," she said softly, her fingers gripping the edge of the shower curtain. "Well, he broke up with me and—"

"*What?!*"

"He broke up with me, Scar." A shrug. "We're done."

Silence. Then, "You don't sound happy about that."

A shake of her head. "That's because I'm not."

"But," Scar whispered, "I thought you guys were perfect for each other."

Great. Now her eyes were stinging again. "I know," she murmured. "Me, too. I um…" She cleared her throat, gaze falling to her feet. "I really liked him."

More silence.

Then Scar was across the room and wrapping her arms tightly around Kacee. "My brother is an idiot."

He was hurting.

She knew that. It didn't make him dumping her, him leaving and not coming back—not even after she'd left him that cabinet on his porch four days before—feel any better.

She was hurting, too.

Because instead of him manning up and talking things through when clearly he felt the same strong feelings about her, when he certainly loved her back because people didn't act like he'd acted, treat their significant others like he had without love being involved, he'd run.

And she'd gone from hurt to pissed off.

Or rather from just hurt to hurt *and* pissed.

"So," she whispered, not taking the bait, even in her hurt and pissed stage, not talking bad about Charlie to Scar. Because that wasn't fair. "I don't think I should come over tomorrow," she finished. "We'll get together another time."

Scar's arms squeezed. "Damn right we will. My brother may be an idiot, but you're part of my Gold family, Kacee. And that means he's just going to have to deal."

"I don't want to get in the way of you two."

"You won't."

"Or complicate things."

"You won't," she said again. "He's the dumbass who's letting the best thing that ever happened to him go."

Now her eyes stung for a different reason. "Scar," she whispered.

"Right." A fierce nod, determination written into the lines of Scarlett's face. "I'm going to fix this."

"Scar." It was a warning now.

"Take your shower," she ordered. "And don't worry," she added with an air of confidence that Kacee definitely didn't feel, "I'll take care of this."

More warning. "Scarlett. I don't think—"

Hands on her shoulders, lightly pressing her back. "Good. *Don't* think. Just take care of yourself, and I'll take care of Charlie."

Now that definitely wasn't a good idea.

"That's not—"

A flick of the shower curtain, zipping across the metal rod, steam suddenly escaping and coating her skin.

"I'll take care of it," Scar said again, more firmly and with a steely determination that had Kacee opening her mouth to protest again.

Too late.

The curtain zipped closed.

Footsteps echoed across the tile.

The door to the hall opened. Shut.

And Scar was gone—or more accurately, Scar had been let loose.

On her brother.

Shit.

Twenty-Seven

Charlie

"What in the fuck all are you doing?"

He glanced up, ignoring his sister for the moment, and instead eyeing the divot she'd created in his wall.

"This is a rental," he said, kneading his pasta dough. "You know that, right?"

"Yup," she clipped, striding across the room.

"Which means that I'm going to have to pay to repair that hole you just made in my wall."

A shrug. "It's a small hole."

She kept walking, moving across the room and making herself at home at his kitchen table. A kitchen table, incidentally, he'd fucked Kacee on.

Brown hair with that hint of blue askew, hazel eyes like molten metal.

And gone now.

Because he'd made that happen. Because he was fucked up and *had* fucked up and—there was just far too much fucked-up happening in his life.

Sighing, he forced himself to focus.

His sister was making holes in his wall, had fire spitting from her eyes, and he needed to brace for Hurricane Scarlett.

"What's up?" he asked. "I thought we weren't supposed to see each other until dinner tomorrow."

"Yup." The P at the end was a pop of sound. An angry, aggressive pop of sound.

"So," he muttered, "just saying that it's not tomorrow."

Her gaze drifted to the clock. "Well," she snapped, "since it's after midnight, I could argue that it's technically tomorrow."

He hated that she was right.

So he didn't reply, just glanced down at the crust he was currently mixing with his hands. On the special cabinet top that Kacee had created for him—because he was a glutton for punishment. "Didn't you request a chocolate pie?"

"Yes, I did."

"Well, not to be a dick," he said, "but I have to work tomorrow. So, if you want this pie, you need to say what you want to say and then get home to your man."

"I want the pie." She crossed her arms. "I want it so that I can share it with Kacee."

Her name sliced through him.

"But, funny story, she told me that you two aren't dating any longer."

He stiffened.

"She *told* me that you dumped her."

His breath was a slow inhale followed by an even slower exhale. "It wasn't working out," he said, rolling out the crust and lifting it to line the tart pan. He cut the excess, used a scrap to press the crust into the edges.

"What wasn't working out?"

He was going to have the most precise pie crust in history. "Scar," he said, "you know that I love you, but this isn't any of your business."

"And you didn't help me get my head on straight with Kaydon?"

A shake of his head. "I mostly gave you a hard time about all the sex you two had while trying not to gag."

"So you're saying that I need to advise you to have more sex until you orgasm enough there's room for your head to fall out of your ass?"

He scowled at her. "Hilarious."

"I love you, Char," she said, "but you're being an idiot. Mom and Dad fucked us up, I get that. But we're not them. We're—"

"This isn't about them."

Her gaze sharpened, and he realized his mistake. He should have just blamed childhood trauma. That was an easier out than trying to explain about Ji-Ho.

She tilted her head to the side. "And I know it's not about Heath," she said softly. "Because you know that he, more than anyone, wanted you to find a person who loved you for the wonderful person you are."

Those words hurt.

Because they were nice, and right at that moment, he didn't deserve nice. He didn't *want* nice.

It hurt too much.

"So, this is about Korea."

He inhaled.

"And why you came home with shadows in your eyes."

"Scar," he began.

"I know you moved there for a relationship," she whispered. Then after a second, "I also know why you didn't tell me."

He didn't even know why he hadn't told her.

"Because if you told me, it became real, and if it didn't work out, I would know that you'd failed and that not everything was okay."

Or that.

Because he'd felt *that*.

"And you're my big brother, and you learned how to be an

awesome one from Heath, but if Heath had one flaw, it was that he held everything so tight to his chest that we didn't know things were wrong until they *were wrong*. He did it with his illness. He did it with the money and food and things at home." Scar's face softened. "And you're like him. You're a wonderful protective older brother, and because of that, you don't want to burden me."

"You had enough hard in your life, Scar, I don't want to add to it." He shook his head, moved to the stove, and started heating his cream for his ganache. "And anyway, I'm fine. Kacee is great, but we weren't right for each other."

"Because you don't think that you deserve to be happy."

No. Because he wasn't going to inflict his *un*happy on her.

His cream was hot, so he removed the pan from the heat and added the chocolate. Then he moved to his mixer, to the heavy cream waiting to be whipped in the bowl, and turned on the motor.

Was it on faster—and louder—than it needed to be?

Maybe.

But did the noise prevent his sister from commenting further?

Yes. For the moment, anyway.

Because the moment didn't last forever, and since he didn't want to make butter (instead of whipped cream), he eventually had to turn off the mixer.

Surprisingly, Scar didn't pounce the moment he did.

Instead, she was silent, and that was almost worse.

Silence as he whisked the ganache, then as he folded in the cream. Silent as he baked the crust and then put it in the freezer to cool. Silent as he filled it.

She didn't pounce until he'd finished the pie.

Until he didn't have anything else to distract him.

That was when she pounced.

"Who broke your heart in Korea, Char?" she asked softly. "Who made it so that you think that you don't deserve to be happy?"

He wanted to be happy.

He didn't want to be a martyr.

He just...it was more important for Kacee to be happy.

Because he loved her.

"It doesn't matter."

Blue eyes on his. "Except it does."

It did, and it didn't. Because it wasn't going to change anything.

"It's over now."

"It's why you came home."

"Sometimes things don't work out the way you want them to," he said softly. "But you have to let go of the dream and move on."

His sister sighed softly, pushed out of the chair. Then she was moving toward him, burrowing her way into his arms and cuddling close. Just like she used to do when she was little. Getting her hair in his face, elbowing him in the gut, the ribs, until she was plastered against him.

Until he hugged her back.

And that was when she stared up at him and delivered a final blow.

"But sometimes, big bro," she said gently, "sometimes you have to fight for that dream."

Twenty-Eight

S he hung up Goldie's head with the rest of her, zipped the deodorizing container closed, and hopped into the shower.

Definitely the best perk of her new Goldie changing room.

So she took her time cleaning off, washing and drying her hair.

God, it felt like it was the first time she'd been clean of sweat, stain, sawdust, and paint in a good three weeks.

Since that night with Charlie.

Because she'd been working to forget, and combined with the long home stretch (and consequence of the team's previous long road trip), she'd been busy.

Busy was good.

Busy distracted.

And busy meant that she was making money. Money was good. Money meant that she'd discontinued the ramen and continued along with the real food that Charlie had stocked for her. Money meant that she'd bought some materials and started making a few items as a thank you for the help at her place—her first iteration of this being personalized cutting boards. She'd think of some other things when she got a little more time.

Plus, she'd babysat.

For Anna and Blue. Then for Blane and Mandy.

And next week, she was watching Emma for a few hours for Coop and Calle so they could go out to dinner and have a little private time.

All that busy and money and taking her sweet time on her hair after her shower meant that by the time she emerged from her changing room, the bowels of the arena were pretty much empty. She nodded and smiled to a few of the support staff as she made her way to the parking lot but didn't encounter any of her friends, not even when she popped her head into the training suite, hoping for a glimpse of Mandy.

Because...delaying.

Because she'd been working so much, she didn't have any projects to distract herself with.

Or more accurately, she had projects, but they were already drawn up, the supply lists ready, and...she didn't have any wood to make them with.

So when she got home to her empty house, there wouldn't be anything to distract her with.

Not even wood scraps, since she'd used those for the cutting boards.

She had wine and popcorn and reality TV.

But that reminded her of Charlie.

And she was really tired of thinking about Charlie. She was *really* tired of thinking about that night and the last few weeks without him. The emptiness and how even though he wasn't in her life, she still felt his presence.

In the pictures.

In the bags of frozen vegetables in her freezer.

In the pristine shine of her tools.

But...he'd made it clear what he wanted, and that *wasn't* a relationship with her. So, she needed to find a way to move on, to be happy, to keep building the ties with her Gold family. Because she wouldn't push herself on someone who didn't want her.

Luckily, the Gold family was happy to include her.

So she was holding tight to that.

Sighing, knowing that she was going to have to go home and face a red wine, popcorn, and reality TV night—even with the shadow of Charlie hanging over her—she started to turn from the training suite.

Then heard a soft curse.

Frowning, she glanced back, saw a flicker of movement. "What?"

She reached for the door, tugged it open, and found...

"Joshua?" she asked.

He glanced up with guilty eyes, hand still in one of Mandy's cabinets.

Her frown deepened, and she stayed in the doorway, hesitant to move closer. What if he was up to something nefarious? What if he was dangerous?

Yeah, he'd helped at her house, but she didn't really know him.

What if he was looking for drugs and she'd just stumbled upon him and...okay, maybe she shouldn't have skipped the reality TV and reminder of Charlie and watched all those true crime documentaries.

He jerked his hand from the set of drawers that Mandy kept next to every treatment table. "I, uh, hi, Kacee."

"What are you doing?"

He cleared his throat. "Nothing."

"Doesn't look like nothing."

He tucked his hands behind his back.

"What are you taking?"

"Nothing."

"So why don't you show me your hands?" She flicked on the lights. "Or why don't you show me what's *in* your hands."

Joshua—and really, it was too bad the man was a thief, because he really *was* pretty. Mocha skin, hazelnut eyes, a sharp jawline that complemented the thick beard he was currently sporting.

And apparently she had a thing for men with beards.

Then again, who wouldn't when they came on sexy men like Charlie and Joshua?

Sighing, he lifted his hands. "It's not what you think?"

She tilted her head to the side. "So, you're *not* stealing supplies from Mandy?"

"I'm—" He sighed, shoulders slumping. "Not so much stealing as trying to self-treat."

That shot her brows straight up to the sky. She was just starting to get to know Mandy, but she didn't think that she would like the idea of one of her players self-treating. "Why would you do that?" she asked.

"Because of *this*—" He turned, lifted the back of his shirt.

She hissed out a breath before she caught herself.

"What happened?"

Slowly, he spun back to face her, and now she watched as his cheeks went slightly red, as his eyes dropped to his feet, and then he shrugged. "I wasn't watching where I was going, tripped over the pack of extra sticks, and then..."

"And then?" she asked when he didn't finish.

"And then I fell into the skate sharpening machine and—" Another shrug. "Um...well, I know it looks bad, but I've had loads of injuries. It's really not that bad at all, and Mandy had already left, so I wasn't going to call her back in or go to the hospital just for a few scrapes."

Those weren't just a *few scrapes,* at least in her opinion, but that was probably less important than, "You've had loads of injuries?"

He cleared his throat, eyes darting away. "I *am* a hockey player."

"Hockey players trip over their own feet and fall into skate machines frequently?"

"Well, it was less tripping over my own feet and more trying to avoid someone."

Now *that* was interesting.

"Avoid who?"

More eye darting. "No one important."

She lifted a brow. "Yeah, so why are you blushing?"

"My skin is brown. I don't blush."

"Maybe not, but your cheeks do get a little pink around the edges." She grinned. "Like right now."

He dug his toe into the carpet.

"Who were you avoiding?"

Silence. But she held her ground. Then he coughed and it was paired with a barely audible sound.

"What was that?"

A sigh. "Christ, you're mean."

For some reason, that made her grin. "Thank you. Now, who's causing the leading scorer this season to nearly slice himself to death? Or should I say, *what's her name?*"

He made a face. Sighed.

Then, said—audibly, this time. "Jess."

"Jess, as in video goal coach, Jess?" Kacee didn't know her well, but the petite brunette was vivacious, sweet, and had a wicked sense of humor.

He nodded.

"So why don't you ask her out?"

A shudder. "She scares me."

This time her brows lifted because how in the world could a five-foot-*if* she was rounding up-two-inch woman scare a six-foot-four giant of a man?

"Joshua."

"Josh, please. Joshua reminds me of my mom yelling at me because I did something stupid."

Her brows did some more talking. Which he saw. And sighed. "Okay, just lay it on me."

"Like stealing supplies because you fell into a skate sharpening machine?"

A scowl. "I hate that you make a legitimate point."

She smiled, bit back a laugh. Her life might be a mess, and she might have declared her love for a man who heard the words and then walked right out her front door, but she hadn't fallen and scraped herself on a skate machine while making a career out of being extremely coordinated. But that was less important at this moment. Which was why she clapped her hands. "Okay then," she ordered. "Shirt off. Ass on the bench."

Concern on his face. "I—um...what?"

"You need those scrapes cleaned, and then you need to come up with a game plan for how you're going to woo one, Jess White."

He sat. "But she's scary," he whispered. "And beautiful. And amazing. And...scary."

She forced back a chuckle. "And so am I with some soap and water."

"Soap and water?" he exclaimed. "But that will burn."

Her brows got another workout. "Got anything better to clean scrapes?"

Another sigh. "No," he muttered.

"Okay, so tell me more about your plan to woo Jess."

"What plan?"

This time she couldn't hold back the chuckle. "Well, shit, Josh. You're in deep, aren't you?"

He sighed—though this time, it was of the lovestruck variety. "Did you know that she built her own computer? And used Corsair Dominator Platinum..."

This, truthfully, was the point she tuned out for a minute, focusing on gently washing his back and slathering it with plenty of antibiotic ointment (all while ignoring the little hisses and moans he made...and seriously, sometimes these giant hockey players were wimps). And kept tuning out, which, in fairness, was probably around the same point people began tuning out her waxing poetic about wood grain.

But she tuned back in when he said, "So then I asked her about her memory"—Kacee didn't think this was of the mental variety—"and she looked at me like I was making fun of her, but I wasn't. And then *I* said that I respected female gamers, and *she* said, 'yeah, probably only those girls doing it while wearing bikinis in hot tubs.'"

Oh boy.

"And I said, 'well, I don't mind those girls in hot tubs, but—'"

This wasn't good.

"—she didn't let me finish because she said, 'Of course, you do,' and then the conversation sort of devolved from there and somehow I was equating female gaming with sex work and, I mean, I'm cool with both because sex work is real work, and I've gotten my ass kicked by enough female gamers to know they're legit, too. But that wasn't what I was trying to say. I just thought she was gorgeous and was excited that she was into something I'm into and—"

He broke off. Made a face.

"And you fucked up."

A nod. "Yup. And now she hates me."

She smoothed some bandages over the cuts and then handed Josh his shirt back. "So, what are you going to do now?"

"Avoid her for all eternity?" he quipped.

"That's not the kind of behavior I expect from the man who's slated to be named captain next year."

There went those cheeks again. "Well, I mean. The guys have to vote, and I'm probably too young..."

"And too modest." She bumped his shoulder with hers. "Josh. You're seriously kickass. Embrace you're inner hockey god. From what I've seen of your play, you'd make a great captain. And the guys already respect you, both the veterans and the rookies. Plus"— she smiled—"confidence is sexy, and paired with that nerdy brain of yours, that jaw that just begs to be rubbed along a woman's thighs"—here *her* cheeks went a bit pink because she could *not* believe she'd said that—"and," she pressed on, "you're nice. She would be lucky to have you. So buck up, come up with a game plan to smooth things over, and then get your ass back in the saddle."

She nudged his hand holding the shirt, and he tugged it over his head. "Did I break you?" she teased.

He smiled, and it was a bit chagrined, but it was also laced with a dash of confidence. "A woman's thighs?" he asked.

Kacee groaned. "I'm not going to live that one down, am I?"

The smile went full grin. "Nope."

She sighed, shook her head. "Well, thank God I have my own blackmail material."

He laughed, bumped her shoulder back. "Yeah, I guess you do." He held up his hand, pinky finger extended. "Friends?"

Warmth through her middle as she lifted her own hand, extended her own pinky. "Friends," she said.

Then they cleaned up, closed down the room, and she knew that she couldn't wait to see what plan Josh came up with to convince Jess to give him a second chance.

Twenty-Nine

CHARLIE

S even more days had passed, and he didn't know what the fuck he was doing with his life.

He cooked and ate, but it all tasted bland.

He hung out with his sister and Kaydon but had a hard time summoning so much as a smile...and even then, it was a struggle because Scar spent most of the time glaring at him expectantly— as though she thought she might be able to glare him into changing his mind.

But it wouldn't work.

He'd made his decision. It was over.

And apparently Kacee was hanging out with Josh now. Scar had told him that little bit of information the night before.

They'd gone to dinner after the game.

And they'd looked "chummy." Scar's words, not his. And he was so fucking depressed that he couldn't even make fun of her for using a word like *chummy*.

Joshua Webb.

Having a breakthrough season. A smile that had sold a million watches—or maybe a few thousand. But the point was that Josh and his pretty face were plastered on billboards around the Bay Area.

He was gorgeous. He was nice. He was big and strong, and Charlie had once watched Josh toss a puck over the glass to a little kid, only to have an adult sweep in and take it. And to pretend to not see Josh indicating he give it back. So Josh had gone to the bench, whispered in someone's ear, then had returned to the ice, making sure the little boy got the puck.

Then a few minutes before the game began, one of the support staff had brought the same little boy a signed jersey.

See?

Nice. Thoughtful.

Perfect for Kacee.

She deserved a man who'd step in for a little boy and turn a sad memory into a great one.

He couldn't make jerseys appear willy-nilly.

He just wanted to rage at women when they declared they loved him.

"Fuck," he muttered, knowing he needed to get his head together. He couldn't keep going in circles like this.

Coffee.

He needed to self-medicate with caffeine and maybe a midmorning stop at Molly's.

Carbs. Sugar. Put some solid time into his plan to gain forty pounds and become a recluse.

Except, he liked people.

He would go crazy as a recluse—even *with* a ready supply of baked goods from Molly's.

Sighing, he pushed up from his desk and made his way to the break room. He needed coffee and he needed it now.

He wove through the cubes, slipped into the break room, the door closing behind him.

A perusal of the cabinet with mugs—he knew he had a couple

tucked in there somewhere, but it had been a bit since he'd partaken in the sludge that was the office coffee. Molly's was close enough that he usually stopped on his way in, or someone made the rounds and brought everyone their order before lunch.

And then, of course, lunch at Molly's wasn't unheard of.

But trying to look at source code while running on maybe eight hours of sleep—over eight days, mind him—meant that he'd slum it with the sludge. He'd just add plenty of creamer and—

Fingers closed over his wrist.

He spun, but not before Ji-Ho was close enough that the rotation brought the front of their bodies into alignment.

"You're avoiding me."

Charlie laughed, broke his hold, and shoved him back a pace and stepped out from between the cabinets and his ex's body. "Of course, I'm avoiding you."

"I don't like it."

"No shit?" he asked sarcastically.

Narrowed eyes, fury sparking to life in dark, dark eyes.

Ji-Ho stepped forward again.

That sick feeling twisted his intestines, shame bubbled, but it was laced with Charlie's own special brand of fury. Because... *enough*. Because this man was the reason he'd ended things with Kacee. Because this *asshole* had broken him, had hit him, had hurt him emotionally and physically, had fucked with his job, had made it his mission to make Charlie's life miserable, and now he'd followed Charlie halfway around the world, just to do that same damned thing all over again.

And worst, he'd left behind a ticking time bomb in his heart, his soul.

And Charlie had *had* enough.

So when Ji-Ho pressed in again, fingers digging painfully into Charlie's biceps, assumed a position meant to intimidate— Charlie lifted his chin. This position had once had *worked* to intimidate. But not anymore.

Because Charlie was empty.

Because he'd left what made him feel full.

Because he was so *fucking* done with this man.

"You know what I do to you when you talk back?"

"I know what I'm *not* going to let you do," Charlie said, glancing toward the opposite wall, toward the flicker of movement, "and that's to keep doing *this*. We broke up, Ji-Ho. You're an abusive asshole who found a weak spot in me and exploited it. But I'm done with that. Let go."

He wasn't going to do that anymore.

Those fingers dug in tighter.

"And I told you that you don't get to decide when we're done. *I* decide that."

No.

Not anymore.

Not *anymore.*

Fuck. Kacee. Her love. Her eyes. Her not being in his life because that *not anymore* was bullshit if he let Ji-Ho define the rest of his life, if he didn't let go of his demons or talk to someone to work through them.

Because he was still giving up everything.

Giving up the treasure he'd been lucky enough to find.

Did he want to live the rest of his life without it?

No.

So he needed to get his own fucking house in order.

"And I'm long past letting you make decisions for me." He glanced down at Ji-Ho's hands, still digging into his biceps, now hard enough that he was going to have bruises. "Let go of me," he gritted. "Or I'm going to make you."

Ji-Ho laughed. It was cruel and terrible, and that cruel and terrible had always been there, so obvious now that he'd had the pure and kind and wonderful of Kacee.

"Let go," he said, seeing movement out of the corner of his eye again. The flash of a door opening. "I've asked you to let go of me three times now. This after I've asked you to stop harassing me at work—" He glanced over Ji-Ho's shoulder, met the eyes of the one person who could deal with this quickly and efficiently. "I have the threatening note he left me. And he's cornered me two other times, getting abusive when I asked him to give me space."

"I saw it."

His gaze drifted to the side, away from Heather O'Keith and to Kels.

"He cornered Charlie in the garage and was threatening him," she said softly. "And I saw the note, too."

"I did, too," Angie said. "Well, I saw the note, and I saw him grab Charlie in here today. And one other time, too."

Charlie's heart warmed.

Maybe he should be feeling shame that these women had seen him in this situation, that they were witnessing the abuse.

But...no more.

This wasn't on him.

This wasn't his fault.

This wasn't *his fault*.

This wasn't...

"My office," Heather ordered. "Now."

Ji-Ho belatedly dropped his hands. "I didn't—"

"My office," she repeated, not looking at Ji-Ho. Instead, she nodded to the security guard who was standing at her side. "*Now.*"

———

There wasn't any judgment on their faces. They'd had his back. Angie had been the one to come into the break room earlier, had seen and understood what was happening. And she hadn't left him to it. She'd gotten Kels and Heather and a security guard.

And now she stood next to his chair outside Heather's office, hand on his shoulder, fingers swinging lightly.

Then she crouched, whispered, "I know this doesn't help, but my dad was an abuser."

He spun to face her, covered her hand with his own. "I'm sorry."

"And I know this isn't easy to accept," she said, still whispering. "But this isn't your fault."

An inhale. An exhale. "I'm realizing that," he said softly. "Too fucking late, but I'm realizing that."

Her expression had been gentle, but at that, it went even more gentle. "Kacee?"

"I fucked up. I thought..." He tilted his head toward Heather's office, where Ji-Ho, the head of HR, a security guard, and Heather had been deep in discussion.

For a while.

This being after the same group—minus the security guard—had talked to Charlie and gotten his side of the story.

Then they'd asked him to wait.

So he had while they'd talked to Kelsey and Angie in turn. And finally, now he was waiting while Ji-Ho was inside.

"You thought you couldn't have something good because he'd taken it all?"

"It wasn't just him," he admitted. "My parents..."

A squeeze of her hand. "I'm sorry."

He shrugged. "It's over now."

"It's never really over," she said. "But the burden gets easier to release when you have someone to share it with."

"Yeah." He sighed. "I'm starting to understand that."

The door to the office swung open and Ji-Ho strode out, the security guard on his heels.

The rage in his eyes was a laser that sliced right through Charlie, but then the security guard moved forward, stepping up and cutting off the line of sight, herding Ji-Ho toward the elevator. Then Charlie didn't have time to watch his ex because Heather was in the doorway of her office, and she was gesturing for him to come in.

She indicated the seat in front of her desk.

He sat and listened to the head of HR discuss what was going to happen (basically Ji-Ho was fired, his access to the building revoked, and they were pulling their support of his work visa). But then he listened with surprise to the report his former supervisor had filed.

No mention of the abuse.

Just that Charlie had put in for a transfer.

And the severance he'd received when he'd initially quit, before they'd offered him this position? Apparently that had been coded in as a one-time bonus.

"I'm sorry," Lana was saying. "If we'd known about the abuse, we never would have brought him here."

"If we'd known about the abuse," Heather said, "he would have been fired. Same as the HR employee you worked with in our Korean office is going to be. And Lana is flying over to vet the entire branch to ensure that this won't ever happen again."

Lana nodded.

Heather folded her hands on her desk. "Lana, can you give us some privacy?"

"Of course," she said. "I need to make my arrangements, anyway." She crossed the room, squeezed his shoulder. "We have counselors available to our employees. I'll email those resources so they're available to you should you decide you'd like to use them."

"Thanks."

A nod. Another squeeze.

Then she was gone, and he was left alone in the office of one Heather O'Keith.

She stared at him.

Silently.

Then she shared. Then she apologized. Then she gave him the space to share what he wanted to share.

And...he did.

And...Angie was a smart cookie.

His burden did get a little lighter when he shared.

And when, after that sharing, Heather turned the conversation to work, to the project he was partnering with Kelsey on, he realized that Heather was smart, too.

She'd given him a safe space to get it out.

Then she'd given him another safe space, one just as equally important.

The space to feel normal again.

THIRTY

KACEE

She sank onto the bench in Brit and Stefan's back yard, needing a quiet minute.

It was Friendsgiving.

Mashed potatoes, dressing, turkeys, Brussel sprouts and green bean casserole, pumpkin and chocolate cream, lemon meringue and pecan pies were stacked on every counter, crowded into the middle of a long table that somehow managed to seat all of the adults.

Then there were the highchairs and the kids' table, the babysitters who'd been hired to give the parents a break and keep everyone happy and entertained (as much as a crew of ten and unders could be kept entertained and happy, which meant there were tears and laughter and spilled drinks and hours of cooking reduced down into the kids eating maybe two Brussel sprouts, a vat of mashed potatoes, and about forty-two dozen dinner rolls).

It had been a blast.

But she was stuffed, having eaten *all* the turkey, *all* the sides, *all* the dinner rolls...and *all* the pies, even though she'd already been beyond full before dessert came around.

And aside from that stuffed, she needed a break.

Because Charlie was there, and seeing him had been painful, more than she'd thought, considering it had been a while, been weeks now and the pain should have lessened. What made it worse?

He'd been watching her.

A lot.

Every time she looked up from her plate, he was there, never in close enough proximity to speak, but his eyes on hers, that longing she'd been trying to work into submission flaring anew. Throbbing and open, yearning and...sad.

She felt sad again.

Ugh.

Now she was sad *and* bloated.

Footsteps on the deck. A male folding himself onto the bench next to her.

But not the male she hoped it would be.

"Hey," Josh said.

She smiled up at him—yes, it was forced, but it was there and that was a victory as far as she was concerned. "Hey."

He settled in, staring up at the sky, and she did the same, liking that he didn't need to fill the silence, that he was comfortable just being there. A good guy. Which was why she turned and asked—okay *teased*, "How's the back?"

A mock-glare. "Better," he said. His face softened. "Thanks to you."

"And your Jess problem?"

Now he winced. "Still a problem," he admitted. "Though we *did* manage to have a civil conversation tonight."

"What, did you ask her to pass the mashed potatoes and she said, 'sure'?"

Silence then, "It was gravy."

She giggled.

"But yes. I even said please."

"And thank you?"

A nod. "*And* thank you."

"Progress," she told him.

"Yeah," he said. "And I'm working on a game plan."

"Does it involve computers?" She'd been in a conversation with Jess that evening, and the other woman was really into them, and especially into the new PC she'd built. Not in an annoying or over-the-top way, but in the way that Kacee was into sharks and wood. It was her jam, and she owned it.

"Yeah."

"She's also into camping," she said. "In case you were wondering, she's dying to get into a campground that's right on the ocean in…" She gave the details of the campground in a sleepy little beach town not far from San Francisco.

Josh slung an arm around her shoulders. "You're pretty freaking awesome, you know that, right?"

"Because I'm a woman with a plan?"

He squeezed. "Because you're a good woman." His voice gentled. "So, how are you hanging in there with Charlie being here?"

His name hurt.

But it was good, in a way, that gossip spread so quickly. News of the breakup had gotten around, and she hadn't had to field any painful questions. Instead, she'd been included in meals and nights out, team events and impromptu gatherings.

Closing ranks.

Supporting.

But still, hearing Charlie's name hurt.

Josh knew it, too. He winced. "Shit, Kace, I'm sorry," he whispered.

A shrug. "It's what it is. Sometimes…sometimes things don't work out, but he helped me realize that I can be part of this"—she nodded to the house—"Gold nuttiness that's wonderful and over-whelming and perfect and the family I never had, but always wanted." Her voice dropped. "He gave me that, and even though we didn't work out, I have that. So I can't regret—"

Now her voice broke, and Josh didn't miss a beat, just tightened his arm and gently pressed her head down onto his shoulder. "The Gold family is awesome," he murmured after a few minutes. "I didn't believe it when I first came to the team. But they're like the mafia. Once you're in, there's no out."

"Except the mafia doesn't welcome more people with open arms."

"True. Unless they're trying to sell illegal training suite supplies."

He chuckled. "Yup. They run a real ring on rolls of gauze and tubes of antibiotic ointment."

"*All* the expensive and classy shit."

Another chuckle then he smoothed a hand down her hair. "Still, I'm sorry about Charlie. It sucks."

It did suck.

But she was used to things sucking. "I can deal."

His palm came to her cheek, tilting her head up. "I know," he said softly, his gaze searching hers. "Just like I know you'll deal with this." He leaned close so that his words puffed on her cheek. "But I'll still be watching through the window just in case you need me."

With that, he was on his feet, her body wavering slightly without the support of his.

She frowned after him, not sure why he was leaving, nor why he'd be watching through the window.

Then she felt *him*.

Every cell in her body perked up. Every nerve realigned. Need coursed through her.

Charlie was there.

Eyes blazing with summer thunderstorms, but his words were calm when he said, "Hey, sweetheart."

Like no time had passed.

Like the gentlest caress.

And God, that hurt.

She started to stand. "Hey," she said once she'd reached her feet, turning for the house, seeing in the square of light that Josh was indeed watching through the window. She took a step toward the back door.

"I'm sorry."

Her feet stalled. Her chest rose and fell on a long breath. "It's all good, Charlie. I get it. Sometimes life gets in the way. Your ex did a number on you. I'm not taking it personally."

Or she was trying not to anyway.

A step toward the door, her hand outstretched toward the knob.

"He didn't just do a number on me, sweetheart. He emotionally abused me." Charlie cleared his throat at the same time she whipped around. "And he hit me. And he sabotaged my job. And...he ingrained this *shame* too deeply inside me."

Now she wasn't going toward the door.

She was moving toward him. "What he did to you wasn't your fault."

"I'm understanding that now. But I didn't for a long time," he whispered, "and when he came here, started working in the same building as me, things got messy, got twisted up in my head. That shame kept bubbling up and choking me, and when you told me you loved me...all of that kind of welled up, and I panicked..."

She waited, but when he didn't say anything else, she murmured, "Love can be scary."

"It was scary because for a second, when you told me that, I... I...almost reacted like he did."

She inhaled sharply, the picture finally clicking into place.

"I almost lashed out at you. I almost *hurt* you and—"

His throat bobbed.

"And when that happened, I knew I couldn't bring that to your doorstep. I *couldn't* do that to you. I couldn't hurt you and —" His shoulders slumped. "Even though I was trying to protect you, I hurt you anyway."

"Why do you think you almost lashed out instead of being able to just talk to me about it?"

"Because the last time someone said they loved me..." His gaze slid away again.

"It turned out like it did with Ji-Ho?"

"Yes." He glanced up at her. "But I understand that now, and I've been talking to a therapist"—a wince—"which is probably not what you want to hear from a man who wants to date you. Having baggage isn't exactly sexy, especially when that baggage caused me to fuck up an important moment where you were making yourself vulnerable and sharing something and I—"

"I don't care."

He blinked. "What?"

"I don't care that you have baggage. I don't care that you need to see a therapist to unpack it. I don't care that your ex messed you up—" A shake of her head. "I mean, I *care* that he did that. Of course, I do. I hate that he hurt you, and I hate that he made wounds inside you that aren't healing." She moved toward him, gently cupped his face in her hands. "Because you're wonderful and you gave me wonderful and I don't care that it comes with things you need to work through because talk about being the poster child for needing help." She smacked a hand against her chest. "I couldn't even ask my friends for help because I was too embarrassed and disappointed in myself for being taken advantage of, for something that wasn't my fault. And I nearly missed out on all the wonderful good inside that house because I was too scared to want it."

"But I left you," he said. "I left you and I was like all the people in your life who did that to you before."

A pulse of pain. "Yes," she whispered. "You did leave." She sighed. "And I won't say that it was easy, because it wasn't. I missed you and it hurt like hell that you didn't march back into my house with groceries and push your way into my life."

His expression locked down, regret dancing in those summer sky eyes.

"But...you also didn't leave."

He frowned.

"You were in my living room, sitting with me on the couch and TV, in the garage with my shining tools, in my hallway with the pictures, in my bedroom with the new pillows and sheets." His beard prickled her hands when he turned his head to the side and kissed one palm and then the other. "So even when you were gone, the evidence of you remained." She cracked a smile. "Haunting me with all the memories."

His fingers wove into her hair. "You want to talk about haunting, sweetheart?" He bent slightly, caught her eyes. "A custom pasta-making table left on my porch like a DoorDash order?"

Her cheeks went a little warm. "I'd already begun it," she said. "And I knew you wouldn't accept it if I tried to give it to you in person."

"No, I wouldn't have," he said.

"Plus, I'm not about to take up pasta-making, not now that I have my personal chef back."

"Yeah?" His fingers pressed into her scalp. "*Am* I back?" he asked lightly.

Her mouth curved. "I don't know, why don't *you* tell *me?*"

The teasing left his eyes. "I want to be back," he whispered. "I want that so badly that I can hardly breathe for wanting you, but you shouldn't just accept me back. You should make me grovel and beg and—"

She kissed him.

Lightly.

Then not so lightly. Because with Charlie, lightly never ended up being light. It went hot and sweet, intense and needy, lovely and like every single piece inside her had shifted into perfect alignment.

"I don't want you to beg," she whispered when she managed to pull away. "I want to be there for you as you work through your past. I want to be your rock and to build you things just because you have a use for them. I want you to hang more photos on the wall and to cook me meals I never could have dreamed of and show me what the world can be when I stop being afraid to live in it." She smoothed her hand over his jaw. "And I want Christmas together and vacations and to be teased by the peeping Toms who are staring out that window at us—"

He whipped around, saw what she'd glimpsed behind his shoulder.

The whole of the Gold gossip train staring at them.

"I want you to be my family," she whispered.

"Fuck, sweetheart," he whispered back.

"Too much?" she asked.

"Too little," he said, wrapping his arms around her and tugging her close. "I promise you that I won't do what I did before. I won't walk away without an explanation. I won't walk away at all—"

"It's okay if you need to," she told him, and meant it.

"Kacee—"

"So long as you come back."

He shuddered out a breath.

"We're not perfect, baby. And I'm fine with that." She rose on tiptoe, brushed her nose along his. "So long as we work on that not perfect together."

He dropped his forehead to hers. "God, I love you."

"I know."

A grin, his hold tightening. "Did you just *Star Wars* me?"

"Maybe," she shrugged, then hitched a thumb over her shoulder. "Okay, yes."

Laughter across the summer sky. A brush of his lips that settled her heart. "I really am sorry."

"I really do know that," she whispered.

"I won't do it again."

"I really do also know that," she whispered again.

"I still feel that I should grovel more."

God, she loved this man. "This isn't an out to treat me like crap. We need to talk through our problems, and if that needs to be with a therapist, then so be it." She tugged his head down to hers, brushed her lips over his lightly once, *twice*. "But I know you wouldn't take it like that anyway," she told him gently, soaking up that warm summer sky, reveling in the gentle fierceness in that gaze, how he held her like she was precious. "*But* if it makes you feel any better, I will require three years of *Shark Week* consumption without complaint as payment."

A brow rose. "Three years?"

"That too many?" she asked.

He brushed his knuckles. "I was thinking you should ask for a lifetime."

"I'm thinking you should ask what's involved in *Shark Week* consumption before you commit to that."

Charlie tossed his head back and laughed, loud and long and the sound filled in all the rough edges, the still-healing wounds. "Fuck, I love you."

"A lifetime then?"

He cupped her cheek. "And that still won't be long enough."

"You might change your mind when you see *Air Jaws 17.*"

More laughter. Then his expression went serious. "No, sweetheart. No, I won't."

She stared into those pretty blue eyes and knew that everything was right in the world, that everything would always be all right so long as Charlie was with her.

A loud bang—akin to the sound of a palm slapping against glass—had them both jumping and turning toward the windows, seeing, yup, even more of the team gathered there.

"Kiss her already!" Josh yelled. "You can talk more later!"

Charlie turned back to her, brows raised. "I'm guessing you don't have to dump Josh in order to give me my second chance?"

She snorted. "You mean dump the big tough hockey player who's in love with Jess? That Josh?"

Charlie's expression went confused. "What?"

"He's in love with Jess...and absolutely terrified of her at the same time."

Charlie grinned. "I know the feeling."

She swatted him and then winced. Because his ex had—

He grabbed her fingers, pressed a kiss to each of them. "Don't," he whispered. "Don't *ever* be anyone but you."

"I love you," she said, leaning close, and knowing that the swat would be her last, whether or not he'd okayed it.

Because he might have made it his mission to take care of her.

But she was going to take care of him right back.

Then because the team was still watching, she kissed *him*.

EPILOGUE

CHARLIE, ONE MONTH LATER

He smiled as he watched Kacee dance her way through the aisles in the next section over, glad she'd suggested that he sit in the stands instead of the box for this last game before the holiday break.

It was a whole different animal being amongst the crowd.

Hearing the cheers reverberate in his stomach, feeling the cool crisp air of the ice on his face. The other noises were clearer too—the claps of the sticks, the thunks of the pucks, the cursing of the players when they made a mistake.

He grinned at Scar, who'd taken the night off and was sitting next to him. "Your boyfriend has a potty mouth."

Laughter in her eyes. "My *boyfriend* isn't just my boyfriend." She held up her hand, and he expected to see a naked finger since the previous season *she'd* proposed to Kaydon—with a plastic Hello Kitty ring, but that was neither here nor there because instead of a naked finger, she was sporting a diamond that could be spotted from space.

"Holy shit, Scar!" he exclaimed, wrapping his arms around her and hugging her tight. "Oh my God! I'm so happy for you!"

"*I'm* so happy for me."

"Good, honey." He tucked her hair behind her ear. "Heath would have loved him."

Her cheeks were pink, her eyes a little glassy, but she nodded. "Yeah, he would have."

The play on the ice stopped, and he left one arm around her, glancing over at Kacee as she boogied with some kids during a commercial break.

Scar saw the direction he was looking—not hard, since he was staring, even though the only parts he could see of the woman he loved were from her knees down. "Heath would have loved her, too."

Now his eyes were a little glassy, but he nodded. "We're fucking lucky, aren't we?"

She grinned. "Damn right, we are."

The commercial break wound down, and he gave Scar another squeeze before hopping to his feet. "I'm going to use the little redheaded boys' room and then get a beer. Want one?"

A shake of her head, her eyes glued to the ice. "I'm good."

Since Kaydon was out there and his sister was staring at him adoringly, he knew that was true. So he pecked her on the top of her head and hurried up the aisle, taking the stairs quickly so that he didn't block the play.

The doors at the top of the aisle were closed, the staff usually checking tickets at the top gone.

But that space wasn't empty.

That space held one person.

One *man*.

Charlie slowed to a halt, time moving in slow motion.

He heard pounding on the other side of the heavy metal doors, probably from the usher trying to get back in. The whistle blew behind him. The music playing began to quiet.

And Ji-Ho—in wrinkled, dirty clothes, his hair a mess, his face a contorted mask, stepped toward him...holding a gun.

Charlie took a step back.

Ji-Ho stepped forward, the bright lights glimmering off the barrel of the gun.

Noise on the ice.

Skates crunching. Players yelling. The crowd shouting.

And he was standing ten feet away from a gun.

"You ruined my life!" Ji-Ho shouted.

The crowd around them hushed. One row and then another and then another. A person nudging another, mouths clamping closed, fear marring expressions, parents covering their children. Other people pulling out their cell phones, filming him.

Filming him about to get shot.

He put his hands up, took another step down, eyes darting from one side to the other.

But there wasn't anywhere he could go.

If he dove into a row, Ji-Ho might fire anyway, and someone innocent might get hurt. Well, he was innocent, too, but he wasn't going to be responsible for someone else being hurt. And if he continued backing down the steps, he would be bringing someone insane closer to the man his sister loved, closer to the men—and women—who had become his family.

He was stuck.

Ji-Ho took the first step down.

Charlie backed down, just one more stair, just one more so that he could have a little more time to think. "Ji-Ho," he began.

"Shut up!"

More rows quieting.

More people cowering in their seats.

More cameras coming out.

"I can fix it," he said. "If you just let me talk to Heather, I'll fix it." He reached into his pocket, pulled out his cell. "I'll call her," he cajoled, totally bluffing but trying for any delay, for anything that would buy him a little more time. "You'll see. It'll be okay and—"

Three things happened at once.

The doors behind Ji-Ho slammed open, a bevy of police officers came running in, guns drawn.

There was a flash of Gold in the corner of his eye.

The arena went completely silent.

And then Goldie—*Kacee*—flew out of an aisle and tackled Ji-Ho.

Hard. Harder than most of the hits on the ice that evening. She collided with Ji-Ho, taking them both to the ground in a flurry of sparkles, gold lamé, and yelling.

Which everyone heard.

Because the arena was silent.

"You!" she screamed, gripping his shoulders and shaking him violently, bouncing his head off the concrete stairs. "Will! Not! Hurt! Him! Ever! *Again!*"

The triangular top of Goldie flew off—probably scarring a child for all eternity. It bounced down the stairs and landed right at Charlie's feet, startling him out of his stunned statueness and having him process exactly what was happening.

His woman. Ji-Ho. A gun. Too fucking close together.

He sprinted up the stairs, reaching her just as the police officers did. They gripped her arms, pulled her off, and apparently the arena's cameras were following the action because the crowd gasped at the same time that he did when seeing Ji-Ho's face.

It was a bloody pulp from Kacee—from Goldie—slamming his head into the stairs.

Ji-Ho was no longer a threat.

That much was clear.

The police closed ranks, separating him from Kacee. The gun was picked up. The fans were told to stay in their seats as the paramedics came and worked on Ji-Ho.

Their eyes locked.

Her color was high.

Tears poured down her cheeks.

He was dangerously close to the same, but he managed to hold it together, and with a whispered word to the officer next to him, Goldie's head was reunited with her costume. The crowd cheered when Goldie was made whole, when Ji-Ho was packed off.

But Charlie didn't have eyes for anyone but Kacee, and when he got permission, he moved to her, took her in his arms, gold lamé, sparkles, and all.

"Ch-Charlie—" She sobbed through the costume.

He shot a glance to the officer. "I'm taking her down below."

The officer nodded, passed him his card. "Don't leave the arena."

"We won't."

Arm around Kacee's waist, he guided her through the now-open doors and onto the concourse, taking her straight toward the elevators.

And in the background?

Cheers of "Goldie! Goldie! Goldie!"

————

"I don't know," she told the officer. "I just...I stopped thinking, and I—"

Her eyes found Charlie's.

He reached out, took her hand. "It's okay, sweetheart. You're okay."

Those pretty hazel eyes were damp. "Not me," she whispered. "You...I just...I saw the gun and you were there and—"

"I think that's enough for tonight," the officer, a young blonde with a slicked-back ponytail, said. "We'll pull the footage, gather the rest of the statements, and reach out if we need anything else, okay?"

"Yes," he said when Kacee just burrowed into his arms.

He'd managed to divest her of Goldie and change her out of her sweaty clothes and then had layered on several Gold sweatshirts, along with wrapping her in a blanket. And she was still shaking.

"Thank you," he said when the officer nodded at him before slipping out the door.

A door, that when opened enough for her to exit, meant that it was opened wide enough for him to see the crowd in the hallway.

"I think you're about to have visitors," he whispered.

Her head rose off his chest, eyes wide. "What?"

"Too late."

Confusion—there and gone, because then the team descended. First, Scar, who was shaking as she hugged them both tightly and then burst into tears (luckily soothed by Kaydon, who held her close and gave her the space to cry it out). Mandy was on her heels with a tub of supplies, immediately taking care of cleaning the abrasions and cuts that Kacee had earned during her heroics. Then came Joshua with a beanie, PR-Rebecca with a pan of brownies, Brit with another blanket, and Cooper with a few packs of ice. And the rest of the team trailed through, all with a kind word or something they thought she might need or assurances that, no, she wasn't fired, and no, it didn't matter that Goldie had gone viral again, for a reason that was definitely not planned.

The most important thing was that Kacee was okay.

Goldie being a hero was a side benefit.

And yeah, so maybe a few kids were scarred because they'd seen the woman inside the costume, but so many others were safe because she'd acted.

And Charlie was, too.

He wanted to give her all the sappy words, and then he wanted to shake her and ask her what the fuck she had been thinking.

But both might make her cry.

And...neither was what she needed.

Which was the attention off her because the thread of her emotions had been strung too tight. She liked the Gold family she'd joined, but she wasn't used to it, and after the scare, after the stress, after everything that had happened, being the focus of so much notice was getting to be too much.

Which was why he threw his sister under the bus. In a gentle way. In a brotherly way. In a way that he knew she wouldn't mind.

"Hey, sissy," he called over the din of fussing. "I think you just blinded me with that diamond!"

The room fell silent.

Then the masses descended.

"Diamond?"

"Holy shit!"

"Engaged!"

"Fuck, man. Congrats!"

And on.

And...the attention off Kacee. Who glanced up at him and smiled gratefully, eyes damp. "Thank you," she murmured.

"*Shark Week*," he told her softly. "For eternity."

One tear slid down her cheek. He wiped it away, held her tight, opened his mouth to give her all that sap—

"I can't wait to show you how high Colossus can jump."

And then they were laughing, and that laughter joined in with the excitement of the engagement, the fight over PR-Rebecca's famous brownies, with teasing and joy, friendship and love.

With the family.

It was imperfect.

It was too damned dramatic.

It was nosy and bossy and sometimes overwhelming.

And...it was home.

———

JOSH

This was it. He had a plan and he was going to do it and it was going to go perfectly, and—

"Jess!"

It was a yell, not the cool, calm greeting he'd intended.

Already imperfect.

Fuck.

She turned slowly, one brown brow lifting. The amount of derision she could impart into that one gesture was truly impressive. "Yeah?"

Double fuck.

"I need to talk to you."

That brow remained lifted, and she shifted on her feet, impatience in every line of her body.

Damn. That had come out as a command.

And Jess didn't like his commands.

He wanted to bet that she'd like them in other places—okay, namely *one* place, that being the bedroom—but they were so fucking far from that possibility it was almost laughable.

God, seriously, how had he *ever* considered himself a player? How had he *ever* thought he was good with women?

Because he was absolute shit with this one.

Or maybe Jess was just the first woman who didn't buy into his bullshit.

He liked that.

He liked that she didn't spread her legs the moment he'd flirted with her—though that probably had less to do with the fact that he'd flirted and more to do with the fact that he'd inadvertently insulted her.

But he liked that, too.

Instead of laughing it off and taking the insult, she'd pushed back. She hadn't taken it. She'd given him...fire.

And fuck, he'd liked it.

He didn't like that he seemed to be digging a deeper fucking hole every single time he interacted with her. Oil and water. Mustard and donuts—was that a thing? Hopefully not because it definitely shouldn't be. Middle-aged white men and power—

Wait.

Shaking himself, hating that he did this shit every time she was near.

Getting lost in her striking blue eyes, wanting to feel the shining silk of her dark brown hair dragging over his skin.

His naked skin.

She spun away from him.

And he realized he'd been staring instead of talking, fucking up instead of following the carefully laid out plan that Kacee had helped him with.

Find out what she needs.

Give it to her.

Don't stop.

He had that figured out. Now he just needed...

To watch her walk away from him.

Shit.

He hustled forward, snagged her arm. "Jess," he said. "Wait!"

She didn't stop, just kept moving toward the parking lot. So, he did the only thing he could.

He stepped in front of her and used his big, broad hockey body to block her path. It was finally good for something—well, *something* that wasn't stopping pucks from getting into the net.

Her brows—both this time—lifted. "Really?" she asked.

"Look, love," he began.

A snort. A repeat of *"really?"* only this time with more derision.

"I know we got off on the wrong foot," he began. "I—"

She laughed. "That's the understatement of the year."

"I didn't mean it that way—"

A scoff. "Oh wow, no surprise. A man trying to excuse his bad behavior by saying *I didn't mean it.*"

Wow, indeed. He filed that away for future pondering. More planning. More puzzling. More figuring out why in the hell she was so prickly.

"I'm trying here," he muttered.

"Oh *wow*," she repeated. "A man who—"

So. Much. Derision.

So. Much. Annoyance.

So much of him wondering why in the fuck all he was fighting for this when she clearly didn't want him.

What was the point?

"—thinks that his *trying* means he can get away with being an asshole."

And...his temper reached its breaking point, splintering along the edges, shooting shards in all directions. He stepped closer, pinning her between his big, hockey body and the wall, bending so that his face was in hers. "*A man*," he growled, "who has been trying for months to get a woman to realize that he likes her and feels like a total shit because he got off on the wrong foot with a woman he's fucking crazy about and a man who has had so many wet dreams about that woman he's crazy about that his fucking balls should be dry."

His chest heaved when the words cut off.

Her eyes went wide, her lips parted.

And for once, she didn't snap back at him.

Instead, she whispered, "Wet dreams?"

That shouldn't make his cock twitch, her reiterating his loss of control. But she was talking about his dick, so he found he didn't really give a shit.

He cupped her cheek, felt his heart skip a beat when she didn't back away. "Yeah, love," he murmured.

Her blue eyes drifted up, locked with his. "You're crazy about me?"

"Yeah, love," he said again.

Those eyes went wide. Then they dipped down.

Toward his cock.

Which twitched again.

And that was the moment that he remembered his plan and the object in his pocket. Which meant that he needed to be focused less on his penis and more on giving her what she needed so that he could win her over, so that he could convince her to give him a chance.

His fingers hit his pocket the same time she straightened and shifted to the side—

And then she shocked the shit out of him by grabbing the tie that hung around his neck, yanking him toward a door, and pulling him inside...

A closet?

"Right," she whispered.

"Jess—" he began.

A yank to his tie before...

Her mouth hit his.

———

Thank you for reading! I hope you loved meeting Charlie and Kacee! The next book in the Gold Hockey series is CAP. Find out if Jess and Josh can stop arguing long enough to realize they're perfect for each other...

She's the one he wants.

And he's not going to give her up without a fight.

CLICK HERE TO READ CAP NOW>

And if you enjoyed CAUGHT, you'll love the sexy, sweet, and close-knit Breakers Hockey crew. The first book in the series, BROKEN, is now live!

It is sexy, hot, adorable and such a fun read. You will not be able to put this down!" —Amazon Reviewer

Her life was a disaster...Don't miss the hilarious Life Sucks series, starting with TRAIN WRECK. Derek Cashette was determined to salvage the train wreck of her life...and she was just as determined *not* to let him be the hero.

DOWNLOAD TRAIN WRECK FOR FREE >

I so appreciate your help in spreading the word about my books, including sharing with friends! Please leave a review on your favorite book site!

You can also join my Facebook group, the Fabinators, for exclusive giveaways and sneak peeks of future books.

SIGN UP FOR ELISE FABER'S NEWSLETTER HERE: https://www.elisefaber.com/newsletter

———

Hate missing Elise's new releases? Love contests, exclusive excerpts and giveaways?

Then signup for Elise's newsletter here!

http://eepurl.com/bdnmEj

———

And join Elise's fan group, the Fabinators (https://www.facebook.com/groups/fabinators) for insider information, sneak peaks at new releases, and fun freebies! Hope to see you there!

———

GOLD HOCKEY SERIES

Gold Hockey **(all stand alone)**
Blocked
Backhand
Boarding
Benched
Breakaway
Breakout
Checked
Coasting
Centered
Charging
Caged
Crashed
A Gold Christmas
Cycled
Caught
Cap

Also by Elise Faber

Billionaire's Club (all stand alone)

Bad Night Stand

Bad Breakup

Bad Husband

Bad Hookup

Bad Divorce

Bad Fiancé

Bad Boyfriend

Bad Blind Date

Bad Wedding

Bad Engagement

Bad Bridesmaid

Bad Swipe

Bad Girlfriend

Bad Best Friend

Bad Billionaire's Quickies

Gold Hockey (all stand alone)

Blocked

Backhand

Boarding

Benched

Breakaway

Breakout

Checked

Coasting

Centered

Charging

Caged

Crashed

A Gold Christmas

Cycled

Caught

Cap

Breakers Hockey (all stand alone)

Broken

Boldly

Breathless

Ballsy (April 26, 2022)

Love, Action, Camera (all stand alone)

Dotted Line

Action Shot

Close-Up

End Scene

Meet Cute

Love After Midnight (all stand alone)

Rum And Notes

Virgin Daiquiri

On The Rocks

Sex On The Seats

Life Sucks Series **(all stand alone)**

Train Wreck

Hot Mess

Dumpster Fire

Clusterf*@k

FUBAR (March 29,2022)

Roosevelt Ranch Series **(all stand alone, series complete)**

Disaster at Roosevelt Ranch

Heartbreak at Roosevelt Ranch

Collision at Roosevelt Ranch

Regret at Roosevelt Ranch

Desire at Roosevelt Ranch

Phoenix Series **(read in order)**

Phoenix Rising

Dark Phoenix

Phoenix Freed

Phoenix: LexTal Chronicles **(rereleasing soon, stand alone, Phoenix world)**

From Ashes

In Flames

To Smoke

KTS Series

Riding The Edge

Crossing The Line

Leveling The Field

Scorching The Earth

Cocky Heroes World

Tattooed Troublemaker

About the Author

USA Today bestselling author, Elise Faber, loves chocolate, Star Wars, Harry Potter, and hockey (the order depending on the day and how well her team -- the Sharks! -- are playing). She and her husband also play as much hockey as they can squeeze into their schedules, so much so that their typical date night is spent on the ice. Elise is the mom to two exuberant boys and lives in Northern California. Connect with her in her Facebook group, the Fabinators or find more information about her books at www.elise-faber.com.

facebook.com/elisefaberauthor
amazon.com/author/elisefaber
bookbub.com/profile/elise-faber
instagram.com/elisefaber
goodreads.com/elisefaber
pinterest.com/elisefaberwrite